Prai... ...

Portrait of an Unknown Lady

A *New York Times Book Review* Editors' Choice

"Gainza has much to say about the creative life, about art and ways of seeing, about perception and reality, authenticity and simulation, fidelity and betrayal. These are matters she takes seriously and about which she writes with exceptional acuity and precision. But the dominant spirit . . . is one of playfulness and humor."
— Sigrid Nunez, *The New York Review of Books*

"The unnamed narrator in *Portrait of an Unknown Lady*, María Gainza's crepuscular but dreamy novel, looks back over a life led in the shadow of imposture . . . The naughty pleasure of this novel is bound up in our fascination with fakes, especially when executed in the cavalier mode of Robin Hood."
— Angus Trumble, *The New York Times Book Review*

"Gainza proves herself a dab hand at concisely digesting artists' lives, finding delight in idiosyncrasy and social rebellion." — Sam Sacks, *The Wall Street Journal*

"A sometimes lush, sometimes minimally inflected—Camus's *The Stranger* comes to mind—tale of a master art counterfeiter named Renee and her bohemian disciples (including the narrator) paints a colorful picture of the Buenos Aires art world of the past century."
—Richard Lipez, *The Washington Post*

"Clever and captivating . . . A richly layered fiction that often limns history . . . Erudite and engagingly digressive."
—Claire Messud, *Harper's Magazine*

"The work of an author in full command of her talents . . . Subtle, incandescent, and luminous—a true master's work."
—*Kirkus Reviews* (starred review)

"This captivating work is one to savor."
—*Publishers Weekly* (boxed and starred review)

"A spare but vivid peek inside a female-dominated environment that's both fascinatingly specific and deeply universal . . . *Portrait of an Unknown Lady* offers no easy answers but provides immense pleasure in the journey to find them."
—*BookPage* (starred review)

"An impressionistic, unconventional, and highly rewarding novel." —David Conrads, *The Christian Science Monitor*

"This tight, eccentric romp through the last sixty years of Argentina's art scene asks pressing questions about the value of art, the nature of reality, and what constitutes an individual after they're gone." —Laurel Taylor, *Asymptote*

"Intelligent and tensile . . . A loose investigation into the nature of art and of memory, scattered with gems of intrigue and insight."   —Emily Temple, *Literary Hub*

"The value of truth, reality, and authenticity are all interrogated in this stunningly slippery novel, as Gainza eloquently probes the difference between art and artifice . . . *Portrait of an Unknown Lady* is wholly original, a quality which things both real and replicated can possess, so long as the creator knows what they are doing. And, with Gainza, readers are in the hands of a master."
                        —Kristin Iversen, *Just Circling Back*

"This metaphysical detective novel offers style, suspense, and quirky character studies that keep you turning the page while you question what it means to make 'authentic' art."   —Rebecca Valley, *Drizzle Review*

"The mutable, esoteric art world is again the setting for award-winning Argentinian Gainza's latest, deftly translated by British writer-editor Bunstead . . . Shrewd audiences will surely enjoy the engrossing challenge of an unpredictable pursuit."   —*Booklist*

"Gainza weaves a fascinating, often confounding story about beauty, obsession and authenticity . . . Like Bolaño, she writes stories within stories, each with its own melancholy mood and unsolvable mystery . . . María Gainza is sharp, modern and playful, a writer who multiplies the possibilities for fiction."   —Johanna Thomas-Corr, *The Guardian*

"A truly exquisite novel . . . Moving, clever and written with a wry precision."   —Stuart Kelly, *The Scotsman*

"An invitation to reconsider what is true and what is false—a touchstone for both the art world and for life itself . . . An exquisite study of representation and the act of looking, a dazzling catalogue of marginal typologies and characters."   —*El País*

"Vividly detailed and saturated with intricate feeling, Gainza's novel is an engrossing exploration of authenticity, obsession, and the enveloping allure of art."
                    —Alexandra Kleeman, author of
                    Something New Under the Sun

"There are many pleasures to be had in reading *Portrait of an Unknown Lady*: its sublime, transcendent sentences, its arch and shadowy figures. Most of all, the zone to which you are transported, which is a Buenos Aires of canvases, trap doors, and dreams."   —Amina Cain, author of *Indelicacy*

Praise for *Optic Nerve*

A *New York Times Book Review* Notable Book of the Year
Named a Best Book of the Year by *Financial Times*,
Hyperallergic, *Publishers Weekly*, and *Thrillist*

"Appealing and digressive . . . María's store of information about painters and their lives can make reading the book feel, delightfully, like auditing a course . . . Consistently charms with its tight swirl of art history, personal reminiscence and aesthetic theories."
          —John Williams, *The New York Times Book Review*

"A roving, impassioned hybrid of art history and memoir . . . The pithy biographical portions of *Optic Nerve* are bracing correctives to potted textbook histories . . . Treat the chapters like stand-alone essays, each one enlivened by the delightful variety and idiosyncrasy of artistic obsession."   —Sam Sacks, *The Wall Street Journal*

"Gainza's long-awaited English-language debut is a provocative novel that investigates the power, value, and emotional significance that art carries, from the perspective of one deeply curious Argentinean woman."

—David Canfield, *Entertainment Weekly*

"*Optic Nerve* would be worth reading as an art history lesson alone; its descriptions of great paintings are phenomenal, as are its lives-of-the-artists anecdotes . . . With each chapter, María finds a new artist to love, and, in doing so, accesses a new part of herself. It's a pleasure to watch her do both."

—Lily Meyer, NPR

"*Optic Nerve*'s episodic iridescence—the way each chapter shimmers with the delicacy of a soap bubble—belies its gravity. Gainza has written an intricate, obsessive, recherché novel about the chasm that opens up between what we see and what we understand."

—Dustin Illingworth, *The Nation*

"Is there anything more exciting than when art defies categorization, resists genre, operates only within the boundaries of its creator's intentions? María Gainza's *Optic Nerve* is one such piece of art."

—Kristin Iversen, *NYLON*

"*Optic Nerve* is one of the best books I've read in years. How did María Gainza pull off something so risky when it never reads as anything less than delightful and engrossing? This is a book that loosens the restraints on literature and gives us a new way of seeing."

—Gabe Habash, author of *Stephen Florida*

"In between autofiction and the microstories of artists, between literary meetups and the intimate chronicle of a family, its past and its misfortunes, this book is completely original, gorgeous, on occasions delicate and other times brutal. And this woman-guide, who goes from Lampedusa to the Doors with crushing elegance, is unforgettable: she knows too much even though she declares herself scatter-brained and unequipped for modern life, even though she only feels alive in front of a secret painting, hiding somewhere in a South American museum."

—Mariana Enríquez, author of
Things We Lost in the Fire

"I was reminded of Berger's *Ways of Seeing* . . . It's so sophisticated and fascinating yet has a Calvino-esque light touch. Rigorous and mercurial."

—Claire-Louise Bennett, author of *Pond*

ALSO BY MARÍA GAINZA

Optic Nerve

PORTRAIT OF AN UNKNOWN LADY

A Novel

MARÍA GAINZA

TRANSLATED FROM THE SPANISH

BY THOMAS BUNSTEAD

CATAPULT

NEW YORK

Copyright © 2018 by María Gainza
English translation copyright © 2022 by Thomas Bunstead
First published in Spain in 2018 by Editorial Anagrama
First published in the United States in 2022 by
Catapult (catapult.co) in agreement with
Casanovas & Lynch Literary Agency

Hardcover ISBN: 978-1-64622-032-8
Paperback ISBN: 978-1-64622-175-2

Jacket design by Dana Li
Cover images: clouds © iStockphoto.com / rudchenko, Lady in a
Fur Wrap (oil on canvas) © Bridgeman / Alonso Sanchez Coello
Book design by Wah-Ming Chang

Library of Congress Control Number: 2021940576

Catapult
New York, NY
books.catapult.co

Printed in the United States of America
1 3 5 7 9 10 8 6 4 2

For Azucena

PORTRAIT OF
AN UNKNOWN LADY

Herself

There I was, finally, at the Hotel Étoile. It said no va-

cancies on the door but I went in anyway and asked for a

room. They gave me one on the tenth floor: view of the

cemetery, Italian marble bath, Louis XVI writing desk,

raft-sized bed the pillows of which were encrusted with little bonbons in burnished wrappers, like rhinestones in the snow. I told the concierge my husband was going to be along later with the luggage, but my husband wasn't ever going to be along. I'm not a person to lie to someone's face but in this instance it was out of my hands.

I checked in under the made-up name of María Lydis. Nobody asked for any papers; had they done so, they might perhaps have recognized the art critic I once was. But with the collar of my mangy black fur coat up around my ears, who was going to pick out the somebody I'd been in the art world, even if it was a fairly prestigious somebody? A claim justified by the idea, however wishful, that a delicate prose style may signify honesty; that style and character are indivisible.

I was going to confine myself to that Imperial Room—so called on the bronze panel over the walnut door—and give free rein to the inner hackette we all bear inside. The only way for me to *turn the page*, to *start afresh*, was to write down what I knew. My model being the eighteenth-century practice among the English, as described in Defoe's *Moll Flanders*, of allowing the condemned to re-count their crimes before being hauled off to the gallows.

Any person reading this ought not to expect names, numbers, or dates. The stuff of my tale has slipped through my fingers, all that remains now is a little of the atmosphere; my techniques are those of the impressionist, and not even the neo- kind. On top of which, my years in the art world have made me wary. I have only distrust for historians coercing the reader with the precision of facts, all those cold, crabbed notes at the foot of the page. "It was so," they say. I am at the point where it is the nicer distinctions I appreciate, and I prefer for people to say, "Let us suppose it was so."

I was born with a skewed smile. A weakness in my muscles means the left corner of my mouth never reaches quite so high as the loftier right. Duplicitousness, people say this is a sign of, an underhand nature—like the good man who turned thief because his shoulders, when he walked, evinced the languor of a cat. And when people say a thing, and then repeat it and repeat it, eventually one does come to believe it. If there's anything that could be said to define the way I am today, it's a general jitteriness. Very early in life, for reasons not to the point, I gave up any hopes I might have stored in either men or women. And in any case, those of my own sex have always been guarded in my presence. There has only ever been one woman who put her trust in me, which made me feel valued, and to people who do that, one owes everything.

We first met in the offices of Ciudad Bank, in the fine

art valuations department. Enriqueta began working there in the 1960s as a *cum laude* graduate of the Argentinean Fine Arts Academy. I had gotten a job through friends of the family, which in my time was the way jobs were got.

At a Christmas get-together a couple of years ago, my uncle Richard stood up and, in a booming drunken slur, announced that what our very own black sheep needed was a job, that it was the only way to whip her into shape. My uncle's intelligence and clichés have always been a good match. A start in the world was the last thing on my mind. In fact, my personal credo consisted of a firm commitment to drifting along, to avoiding ties with anyone or anything. In the family, however, I was deemed a lost cause, and the best I could hope for was to excel as a catcher of butterflies. I don't know why exactly, but for some reason I decided to accept the challenge. Probably to shut Uncle Richard up. So it was that a drunken conversation led to me starting work as the personal slave of Enriqueta Macedo.

It was nine o'clock in the morning on the first Monday in January when I opened the glass door at Ciudad Bank and approached the female receptionist sitting on the far side of a glass counter. She wore no bra, for all that that particular battle had long since been won, and when I said

Señorita Macedo was expecting me, her raised eyebrows suggested that a mauling was not beyond the realms of possibility. She directed me to another glass door. The prevalence of that material stood out to me; an attempt perhaps to give the impression of transparency in the dealings of the institution it housed.

There was no need to ask whether she was she. Enriqueta Macedo was the country's preeminent expert in art authentication, a true great of the art world, and when I went in I found her crouching close up to a painting on the wall, about to dive into it. She didn't so much appear to be looking at it as to be taking in its scent. I cleared my throat, timidly, like people in the movies. She got to her feet, surprisingly supple for a woman her age, and raised her chin to beckon me. (This haughty gesture, I later realized, was a way of lifting her sagging neck skin.) She wore a lemon-yellow blouse and a creased, steel-gray trouser suit. On the outside unremarkable, a touch preposterous, even, but, as I would later realize, it was an exterior to belie what lay within.

I immediately did as instructed and went over. There was something of the hospital scanner in the way her eyes looked me up and down. Since I found it impossible to hold her gaze, I opted to look at my feet, just black blots on the floor. She spoke before I had a chance to think.

"Well, I hope you've done your homework."

I flickered one of my lopsided smiles at her, the asymmetry of which might have amused, pained, or come as a relief to her. Enriqueta gave a commiserative click of the tongue and led me over to her desk.

"Don't mind my little games. Always looking for a fight! Seems I can't help it. Now," she said, indicating a pile of twenty or so black folders, "your first assignment. Family secrets."

Like a frock coat worn to conceal a belly too big, the folders held the invoices for every painting deposited with the bank over the course of several months. I began looking through the seemingly endless paper trail, and, when I grew weary of feigning interest, resigned myself to my fate. I would get used to it, I said. It's remarkable how quickly we can get used to anything.

I was twenty-five and had landed a job in the most distinguished valuations department in the country: the single, despotic authority on the price and authenticity of all paintings then being bought or sold across the land, and a kind of upmarket pawnshop and storage-space provider any time there was a legal dispute over an artwork. Despite any apparent mystique, from the inside it was a darkly governmental kind of place, soul-sapping in its grayness.

A diffuse sensation of distress occasionally gripped me.

All the talk was of profit margins, and the employees spoke a language I could only partially follow—as though just the single units of speech, never the overall import. In order to establish a place for myself in this money-worshipping family, I assumed a rather questionable attitude: I made my contempt for money clear.

Only Enriqueta seemed to comprehend my moral asphyxia. The time that has now elapsed makes it difficult to do justice to her, but let us say that in her I found all the flair and grace otherwise so seemingly lacking in this new environment.

She was the kind of woman whom old age suited. At last!, she must have thought. In winter she wore a black fur coat that had something of the mangy dog about it. It was far from fetching, but it kept the cold off and that was all she cared about. You would see her arrive at the office, an air of divine severity about her, perhaps the product of so many years spent in close quarters with works of art. These paintings are like the mountains, I remember her saying once as she looked around her, they will outlive us all.

Enriqueta was clear-eyed when it came to people but her faith in art bordered on the esoteric. She rarely spoke of it, but then she was of a generation that had less need to verbalize absolutely everything. Her work hours were spent in a no-frills office, the furniture upholstered in real leather and framed reproductions of William Blake prints on the walls. On that first day, seeing me eyeing them, she invited me to take a closer look.

"But careful," she said, "they bite. Or they could if they wanted to. They're all I believe in."

They were from Blake's *Paradise Lost*. The scenes of hell struck me as far superior to those set in heaven, though I did not say so. I was yet to learn what it meant to have an opinion of one's own. The day would come when it would cost me to think for myself.

There was an air of mystery in Enriqueta's office: it would have been little surprise to see one of the book-lined walls swing open to reveal a hidden corridor. She sat at her desk, head poking out from behind catalogues piled up around her like a wagon circle. Her origins were always unclear. She never mentioned her family, save to recall a great-grandfather who was among those depicted in *The Raft of the Medusa*, and who suffered the fate of being eaten by the other castaways. Apart from this honorable genealogical detail, she moved through life as if alone.

She was cold and severe and, in the eyes of people in the office—the normal sort of people one finds in offices—pompous too. Yet I took to her in an instant. And not only because working under her was a training for the mind, but because something told me she was more than a mere upper-class monster. A rare soul, you might say, one of the initiated. And possessed of the raptor's eye—a thing like gold dust in that milieu, and increasingly so, like a clinical eye in the world of medicine. She could look *through* a picture; see its whole matrix. She had an innate skill for deconstructing an image in her mind and putting it back together again, as a Swiss watchmaker would a clock. Also an avowed Luddite, she rejected out of hand any technological advance claiming to assist in the work of authentication. The only thing she permitted was a flashlight, small enough to fit in the palm of one's hand, that emitted a bluish glow barely visible to the naked eye. The black light, as it is known in forensic science, used at crime scenes to detect traces of blood, semen, saliva, or sweat. What art authenticators are looking for with it are the final additions to any work. According to Enriqueta, this little device was all one needed to delve into a painting's core. Nothing else was worth the trouble.

How long would it take a woman like Enriqueta to see through me? A month? A week? Perhaps a few minutes would do it. But to my great surprise, it seemed she saw something in me: she immediately decided to take me under her wing and, before I had realized it, chose me as her successor.

"Mark my words," she said a few days in. "Never let your emotions show while you are between these four walls. Keep your cards close to your chest and they'll leave you be."

Wanting to make me more unflappable, she told me the story of Anaxagoras, the pre-Socratic who, on learning of the death of his son, replied, *"Sciebam me genuisse mortalem"* ("I knew I had begot a mortal"). And yet I am sure her serenity, which she hoisted like a flag of philosophy, wasn't her natural disposition. It was her method, I believe, of keeping the world at bay.

My first months were a crash course in all that goes into the valuation of a work of art. I was young, I knew little, and the little I knew I didn't understand, but at the same time I was liable to be interested, voraciously interested, in just about anything. I hung on Enriqueta's every word and, in a hardcover Rivadavia notebook, wrote down the pearls she dropped along the way. Headings such as: "Establishing pedigree"; "Origin, authenticity"; "Differentiating old canvas from tea-stained paper"; "Minor details: ears, fingernails (Giovanni Morelli technique)." It was rare that Enriqueta came out with anything that was not both as pointed and as pleasingly formed as a hedgehog. She often spoke in aphorisms, and made no distinction between those borrowed and those she herself made up: "A conversation about a painting is the quickest way to get to know a person." Or, "It is best to be bursting for the toilet when viewing a painting: a sphincter on the edge makes for an alert mind." Or, "Art is the greatest way to find out what people are truly like. It is the cheapest lie detector I know of." She needed no prompting to come out with such things.

On Fridays, always the quietest day of the week, she sent me to the library for old auction catalogues, and I was then to spend the day poring over them. "This is a muscle," she said. "And it needs building up, like any other." I looked without knowing what I was supposed to be looking at. When, in desperation, I pointed this out, she said, "A moment comes when you just know. You feel it, or sense it: what a piece is supposed to look like." Her talk about paintings often seemed to teeter into advice on the art of living.

Another thing about her: there was an acuteness, an aliveness, in everything that she did. To me, whether I was helping her with the crossword, removing the bones from the fish she was about to eat, right up to tying her shoelaces when her arthritis was bad, all was pure poetry.

Come 6 p.m., when most of the staff disappeared, the two of us would go up to the rooftop terrace to continue the conversation. I had the best seat in the house for these twilit disquisitions of hers. She could hold forth for hours on Vasari, Karel van Mander, Pico della Mirandola, though always eschewing the leaden solemnity of the academy; eyes closed, she spoke of these artists as lifelong intimates, referring to them by nicknames of her own devising, or upbraiding them for their lack of hygiene. It seemed to me like she forgot, for whole moments at a time, where she was and with whom. But there were days, if the sky was clear as the sun went down, when a rare combination of solar radiation, smog, and the neon signs bathed the cityscape in a light the color of roasted apples, like something out of a painting by the Pre-Raphaelite Edward Burne-Jones. I am talking of an optical effect lasting no more than five minutes but which would, the moment it began, see Enriqueta leap out of her lounge chair like bread from a toaster, look to the sky, and, pursing her lips, murmur, "*Flammantia moenia mundi*," at which, the coppery light striking her chest and pouring down over her shoulders, a prolonged shiver ran through my body. Suddenly I saw her for what she was: an artist who had never produced a work of art; a work of art in her own right.

I very soon made it clear that I was at her disposal for whatever she should need; whether it be making coffee or carrying out an act of cold-blooded murder, she should do with me as she pleased. Enriqueta read me like a book.

•

I had been at Ciudad Bank for a year when I got up one Sunday morning to an answering machine message saying I was to meet her at 5 p.m. on the corner of Suipacha and Sarmiento, and to bring my swimsuit. Like the good soldier I was, I readied my kit and, approaching the appointed address, was reminded of the line about a person's character being formed on Sunday afternoons.

She was there when I arrived, standing in the doorway smoking one of her Gauloises—always smoked to the final millimeter, always dropped to the ground and crushed under her French heels. She gestured for me to follow her—such intimacy in that gesture! "Commit a crime and the world turns to glass," she murmured, eyes flicking left and right as we entered the Colmegna baths. The people working there, with their flushed faces, peremptory manner, and white uniforms, greeted her like a lifelong acquaintance.

In the airless changing rooms I put on my swimsuit, the Lycra baggy, and made my way out to a pool around which firm-bodied sirens and sea gods had once frolicked, but that now stood in a state of semi-abandonment, the tiling loose underfoot. A cluster of elderly men and women, skin sagging, sat on the edges dangling their feet, harboring loneliness and fears.

Enriqueta appeared a few minutes later, looking unexpectedly stylish in her black swimsuit and gliding down the metal ladder, moving as fluidly as a signature's flourish, to join me in the tepid water. We silently swam some breaststroke. Another truth: strong winds will keep you away from those of your own species, but water joins you together.

We got out, wrapped ourselves in the rough white towels, and, like Carthusian monks, went down a passageway sticky underfoot with grime. We came to a small wood-paneled room, the steps and platforms wooden as well, a hint of rosemary on the searing air. We sat down facing each other and then, seeing as nobody came in, turned over onto our backs. It was a good place for not saying anything. Outside the sauna, the elderly group had begun to make their way around the edge of the pool, and the high-pitched creaking of their walking sticks and Zimmer frames could be heard, a strange sound, as though those contraptions were made of ice. I started to feel like my head had a wool blanket wrapped around it and soon fell into something of a daze.

"Now, if you don't mind," said Enriqueta, jolting me out of my stupor, "I am going to tell you one or two things. Things I want you to know."

The anecdote about Garibaldi on his departure from Rome came to mind, saying to his men he could promise thirst and heat by day, cold and hunger by night, and great danger at all hours. The usual hoarse concision of her speech was gone. Her voice grew distant, as though she were addressing me from horseback, or from high on a mountain, and in a language that in other circumstances I would have defined as biblical. I can make little claim for fidelity in my tale, given how my relaxed muscles conspired against my ability to concentrate, but at the same time I know very well the crux of what was said.

For a span of forty years, Enriqueta Macedo, upright and beyond reproach, had been giving certificates of authenticity to forged works of art. She earned a commission from each spurious piece that she authenticated, but money was not what drove her. Rather, she said, she wanted to raise the bar for art in general: the true measure of a painting, she said, was how good it was, not the accuracy of the signature in the corner.

"Can a forgery not give as much pleasure as an original? Isn't there a point when fakes become more authentic than originals? And anyway," she added, "isn't the real scandal the market itself?" All of this she fired at me point-blank, with no expectation of any reply. She was

Enriqueta Macedo, the "Herself" of the valuations department: how on earth could I be expected to find fault with her arguments?

That first conversation lasted no more than twenty minutes, the recognized period of time after which it becomes very tedious to stay in a sauna. But we found our way back there again on several occasions. It quickly became clear to me why kingpins in the criminal underworld choose to run their private affairs in such places; even the most committed informer, reduced to a swimsuit, can't wear a wire. O sauna! O great leveler! With bellies on display, there is nothing to tell the millionaire from the beggar, the low-down criminal from the most distinguished of citizens.

From then on, important matters were always discussed in that small, hot cubicle. There were times when the billowing steam grew especially thick and, the figure of Enriqueta apparently vanishing, I felt that I was actually alone, and that the voice I could hear was coming from inside me.

Simply put, this was my entry into the world of crime. I finally felt part of something, and the two facets of myself felt met—the one that yearned for protection and the other, always in need of adventure. Naturally fear got the better of me at times, and I hadn't yet found my way to the right philosophers in order to know that all strong sensations bring with them a certain amount of terror.

It soon became clear that she and I were identical souls disguised under different identities. *Unsereiner*, Enriqueta said we were, quoting the great Bernard Berenson. At root, we were two romantics, rebels to the bourgeoisie and to that whole way of seeing the world: the buying way.

With Enriqueta, my life was no longer bland and flavorless. We would spend evenings at her apartment on Pasaje del Carmen eating scrambled eggs (the secret to which, she showed me, was enormous quantities of butter) and watching Orson Welles's *F for Fake*, a documentary film that is to the world of art forgery as *The Godfather* is to the Mafia. Elmyr de Hory, the most notorious forger of the twentieth century, was our very own Vito Corleone: the first person to transform the criminal experience into something complex, noble, and heroic. It never failed to leave us rapt, with some new detail emerging for discussion with every viewing. It was also always the same scenes that made Enriqueta laugh, a sound like vast amounts of coal rumbling down a chute; it was a sound from another world, and diabolically contagious.

The forgers we used had little in common with de Hory. They tended to lead obscure lives, often as graduates of the Fine Arts Academy who'd failed to break into the art scene and worked other jobs by day. There was Crosatto, plumber and specialist in Butler; Chacarita, with his job in his family's car workshop and his unerring Quinquelas; Suárez, who was in fact a successful artist but one who, out of a natural transgressive bent, painted Macciós that were—in his words—"better than the real thing," and who had the whole Harte family on the production line; and Mildred, a former hostess at the Dragón Rojo, legendary for having forged the Magritte held in the Klemm collection. All were good, said Enriqueta, consummate, even, but none had what she once saw in a forger called Renée: "The disconcerting ability to enter the soul of another." It was the first time I heard the name.

We would meet the forger in Las Delicias, a bar on the corner of Callao and Quintana, at a table at the back on the right. We would be accompanied by Lozinski, the Russian who acted as intermediary but who said next to nothing, intent instead on doodling on a paper napkin for the entirety of each meeting. He and Enriqueta acted like old friends, though the past was never explicitly mentioned. There would be gin and tonics, there would be bar snacks, and once the niceties were out of the way Enriqueta would place the envelope containing the certificate of authenticity on the table, swiftly met by one from the forger

containing the money. These were slid in opposite direc-
tions, like passing cars. Then it would be into the ladies'
to count the money. Enriqueta's practice was to make two
rolls of a similar size, undo the top button of her blouse
and insert each into her bra. And every time without fail,
doing her button up and checking her appearance in the
mirror, with breasts newly bolstered, she would blow on
the tip of her forefinger like the smoking barrel of a gun.

I felt great kinship with Enriqueta, but at the same time
began to wonder: Was it in fact with her, or with my own
way of thinking? Enriqueta expressed all that I admired,
with the difference that she also embodied it. Nobody in
the office knew but us. "These things are done either dis-
creetly," Enriqueta would say, "or not at all." Though really my part was a minor one; it was a *delectatio morosa* sort
of thing, me as sidekick, or voyeur if one prefers. So if it
was raining, let us say, it would fall to me to hold the um-
brella above her head all the way to whichever assignation
we were bound for, and when the rain stopped, carefully
close it, shake the raindrops off, and hook it over my fore-
arm for the rest of the way. The substance of our activities,
the Rolodex and the phone calls themselves, were her do-
main. There were occasions when we would come out of
a meeting and I would catch her observing me—trying to

establish the thickness of my skin, I think. But for all our shady dealings, there was never any point at which I felt shocked. It was not that Enriqueta set me on the path to corruption, more that she revealed how far along it I had already gone.

There would also be weeks when no forgeries came in, and that saw the two of us at odds with the world, and me submerged in the endless barrenness of paperwork. But eventually a piece would arrive, and it was like the blood returning to our veins. "It has a certain *je ne sais quoi*," Enriqueta would say, rubbing her hands together like a squirrel on the way to make mischief. "A pleasure that's hard to describe, no? Wars have been started, and homes broken, and careers ended just for this very feeling."

The two of us were due to spend a weekend at the Gualeguaychú hot springs when, on the Wednesday before, Enriqueta did not turn up at work. She had not missed a day in years, and Uncle Richard suggested I walk over to her apartment during lunchtime. I knew I would be able to get in, given my knowledge of the coin trick, a secret I unfortunately cannot divulge here.

Going into the bathroom, I found her lying on her back on the white marble floor. The tap in the sink was running. She was wearing her yellow blouse and gray skirt, and compression stockings covered her sturdy lower legs. I was granted a view of her hairline, far back on the forehead like a disobedient glacier gone drifting far, far upstream. But, this minor irregularity aside, nothing looked out of the ordinary: there was neither blood nor the smell of rotting flesh, nothing dramatic. She had gone into the bathroom, it looked like, to get a glass of water. She was hardly the picture of health, having suffered from esophagitis for forty or so years, relied on only the one kidney for about thirty, and coped with rheumatoid arthritis for the last three. Whatever had killed her, it had been quick: something tells me she would not have known the end was coming. Her birthday was the following week; she would have been seventy-seven.

Quite a long time I stood there not knowing what to do. A gamut of unfamiliar feelings ran through me, feelings that no combination of material and movement could hope to express. At some point I turned off the tap and went back into the living room, but that was worse: there you could hear the gurgling of the pipes, and it was as though a mournfulness had installed itself in the gullet of the building. It was the first time I had picked up on the air of poverty in that apartment, something ramshackle in spite of the tidiness of it all. An unpainted wooden bed that acted as an armchair, two old wicker chairs, and, where the walls should have been, row upon row of books. An interior as unfussy, and as utterly lacking in any hint of sentimentality, as Enriqueta.

It was then that I saw the fur coat hanging on the back of the door. It seemed clear that I was its owner now, and when I tried it on, reaching into one of the pockets, my hand alighted on something metal. I took it out. Turned it on. The faint bluish light seemed to glow brighter than ever, though doubtless that wasn't really so. I collapsed on one of the chairs and began to cry. Those tears were over many things, some of which had nothing to do with Enriqueta; such is the way with any bout of that kind, dragging forgotten jetsam along with it like the water pooling around a patio drain. I fell asleep then, though it must have been for only a few minutes: indeed, in the very same moment as doing so, I woke again. I picked up the phone and made the necessary calls. Within hours the various professionals who make a living from the dead had launched into action, and I had become superfluous.

The next day I was standing at the entrance to Chacarita Cemetery when a woman approached me, her threadbare espadrilles flapping against the flagstones. It was as cold as Siberia, but she appeared entirely at home in the kind of harsh climes where nobody else would choose to set foot, the sort of woman who comes into her own when others are suffering. She was the cemetery warden and it was clear from her unblinking expression that empathy was not within her capabilities.

"I'm short-staffed," she said. Her name tag said "Paz" in red lettering that had clearly been bright once but had now lost all conviction. "All my caretakers have been laid off. We had a looting the other day, one of the crypts— they took everything."

A man with a gray, pointed beard materialized under a nearby cypress, nodding at me severely. It was the Russian, faithful Lozinski. In full military dress, with knee-length green jacket and high cherry-red boots, he had a wreath made of white lilies that can't have been cheap. Roses had been selling at a reasonable price, and carnations hadn't been too bad, but white lilies were Enriqueta's favorite and this was not the moment to be tight-fisted. Flowers are important, said the Russian, coming over. When Prokofiev died, he said, all the flower stalls in Moscow were bare. They'd been cleaned out for Stalin's funeral, every single stem. A sad story—it had a ring to it. Did that make it true?

A quarter of an hour later, the warden opened the chapel doors—just as the funeral car was pulling up. We went inside: Lozinski, some people from the office who had turned up at the very last moment, Uncle Richard, and me. The coffin was on its stand by the altar. The warden led the way down the aisle, lighting the candles on either side. If her intention was to warm the space, there was little point, given that the sun was pouring in through the stained-glass windows as if through giant magnifying glasses. Sooner or later we would all be ashes.

The priest spoke on the generosity of mercy, and about sadness and pain, and hope and love. A touch of everything. Lozinski approached the coffin and I fell in behind him. Enriqueta's dead lips were painted a garish red and the lace cap framing her face would have struck her as very *démodé*, and yet a self-assurance still emanated from her. My dear friend seemed to know where it was that she was going, something that had always been part of her charm for me. Following Russian tradition, Lozinski had brought a pair of old coins and placed them on the deceased's eyelids, before saying, "May your influence go forth upon the air."

Then the funeral director came forward and lowered the coffin lid and we proceeded to a grave that had been dug at the end of an avenue of lime trees. A gardener was trimming around the edge of some nearby gravestones but seeing us approach turned the machine off and bowed his head to wait. Once the coffin had been lowered, all present dropped in a handful of the rubbly soil; the interior of the grave looked chill and muddy to me, and

I thought how it would be a matter of weeks before the coffin wood rotted and my friend's body was at the mercy of the worms below.

I just wanted the whole pantomime to be over. Perhaps Enriqueta had catalepsy. Should we not have laid a red-hot brand against the soles of her feet, as was advised in former times? And if she did not wake up, well, *then* let the burial continue . . .

The priest said a few further words, simply to fill the gap—or rather the yawning emptiness that I, at least, felt inside me. I caught sight of a taxi in the distance, on the far side of some trees; it looked as though it was waiting to collect somebody. Then I saw, or I thought I did, some binoculars poking out of the rear window. I was about to say something to Lozinski when the tinted window wound up and the vehicle swung around and drove off. I then saw the Russian's back trembling with small convulsions, and I could think of nothing to say to that old man crying by my side.

The trimmer came back on, signaling an end to the proceedings. I walked away in true French style—that is, without a word. I later learned that Enriqueta had left the burial money sewn into her curtains. The police found it when they were inspecting the apartment.

•

I fell into life.

When John O'Hara received a phone call from a friend telling him about George Gershwin's death, the poet shouted into the receiver, "If I don't want to believe it, I don't have to!" But I did believe it. When days pass and the person does not come back, what choice do we have? In the office, everything was completely back to normal that same afternoon. For a time I went on with the same charade as ever. Work, I proposed, would be my way of combatting the terror and solitude.

I took consignments, I ordered catalogues, I answered the phone, I made sure to take the stairs on my fifty trips down to, and back up from, the depot each day. I forced myself to keep moving, wanting to numb my heart by dint of physical tiredness. I played my role to perfection, and yet I still don't know who I was trying to fool. I was exhausted, somewhere between this world and the next. It was as though a blowtorch had been applied to me, and yet the charring had happened only on the inside. The physical building of me was still standing, and yet inwardly there was nothing but static circulating around empty caverns.

I avoided going into her office, which felt like a shrine to me. Does idealizing someone simply mean seeing things nobody else sees? Perhaps if she had hung around a little while longer, cracks would have begun to appear. But as it was, she made her departure just at the right moment, leaving such a gaping crater behind that ideas which previously I had entertained only jokingly became incontestably true. Enriqueta became my model of perfection, my ideal mentor, and, yes, a replacement mother. The moment she died, a sliver of ice was left lodged in my heart.

Melancholical Forgers, Inc.

There is a point in the eye of a hurricane where all is silence.

I went there, and stayed. Enriqueta's world appearing before

my eyes in fleeting bursts, me staying just where I was.

·

A few blocks from the train station in Belgrano R, one house stood out as being more crumbling, prouder, than all the rest. Once a family residence, its owners, hoping to stave off the building's complete collapse, had turned it into a hotel. They named it the Hotel Switzerland, thinking the Helvetian allusion would attract wealthy guests, but the combination of the bindweed choking the entrance, the creaking gate, and the blackened marble steps generated a distinctly antique air, one of melancholy and adventure. Unsurprisingly, it was tatty bohemians who ended up flocking there.

It was in the small hours of a gin-and-cigarette-fueled night that the guest in the room at the end of the corridor, a poet and romantic named Máximo Simpson, rechristened it the Hotel Melancholical:

The Hotel Melancholical
sails deathwards through the night
with its black hallways plied
by Tsar Alexander's distant marshals,
with its old samovars and gloomy
    demijohns,
with its cracked floor tiles and tattered
    armchairs;
spent autocracy, venerable patina.
Little archaeology of the poor hostel dweller
conserving half a soul amid the ruins.

Some of the long-term residents claimed they spent their happiest days there. Rose-tinted spectacles, perhaps. Unless of course such a thing does exist, *the happiest days of our lives*. Which in itself would be fairly dispiriting.

The hotel comprised two separate buildings with an adjoining garden of cypresses. In the building facing the street lived the Russian manageress, Madame Maria Yvanovna Vadim, dressed always in her careless finery. Her father was a tsarist general who escaped to Prague during the Bolshevik Revolution, succeeding in getting his wife and daughter out too. Husband and wife both died soon after, and Maria Yvanovna, their only daughter, was suddenly old: nothing ages a person like the death of their parents. She could just as well have moved on to Alaska, but the next boat sailing from Europe was bound for Argentina. Maria Yvanovna watched as her home continent slipped out of sight and after that never found anything approaching happiness again, though she did go to some lengths to avoid despair. In Buenos Aires the only friendship that provided a link to her past was with a young ex-admiral named Lozinski, stationed with the Vladivostok fleet. They had met at the porteño cabaret Chez son Altesse. The admiral would arrive at the hotel after siesta and walk Madame Vadim arm in arm through the gardens. She liked to stop at the *Mimosa pudica*—also known as the shameplant or touch-me-not for the way it simulates death on contact, folding inward and drooping, reopening only once the onlooker has moved on.

Guests stayed in the other building, at the far end of the garden. Artists and inamorati to a one, they spent their days sprawled on fraying armchairs, and the talk at the Hotel Melancholical worked on them as the music did. They were invariably intelligent and talented, and never destined for much. Politics were not spoken of and there was a general rule of leaving one's shoes out on the landing. Madame Vadim had adopted the custom of Russian galleries, where visitors were obliged to put on felt slippers so as not to scratch the parquet.

The hotel gate is open. Enriqueta catches her toe and half-trips on a hose someone has left unrolled at the foot of the front steps. A less dignified beginning than she has been hoping for, but nobody sees. She rings the bell and the carved walnut front door swings open; and in it stands a figure. It is Renée, flinty eyes lined with kohl. Her skin is black, not the brilliant black of Africans but an opaque black, as though the sun has absorbed all possible reflection. Her worn red sweater is covered in cigarette burns, and her gray wool trousers are elegantly, unexpectedly finished by a black crocodile-skin belt. Not the sort of look you would have seen in *Hello!* in 1963—that would have meant hair teased up, perhaps a beret, fur collar, pencil skirt—but the ensemble fits so perfectly, hugging the contours of her body, that it's almost as though the best seamstresses have joined forces especially to provide the outfit.

"You! That's a surprise. You'd better come in."

It is a tug Enriqueta knows already, between the wish to remain on the shore, all alone, and the desire to be dragged to deeper waters. Renée takes her arm and brings her inside. At least so Enriqueta would later claim.

Who are all these people? They look like a second-rate secret society, a gallery of characters joined by what might be called fortune or chance. Enriqueta is introduced to the company, and gives a bow when they come to the manageress, the redhead with matching fake ruby glinting on her pinky; at her side is the former admiral, Lozinski, in threadbare military green.

"Madame Vadim, let me introduce my golden girl."

Everyone in the room turns to look.

A mad trumpet starts up from a stage nestled in back. The men are in dark suits thin at the elbows, white open-necked shirts, and their hair is shaved very short at back and sides. A poet with a mono-brow, notebook before him on the fireplace grate, intones his verses; there is an ex-Communist yapping about the world of publicity with the desperate energy of a lapdog; another man, curly-haired, the definition of raffish, goes around speechifying about a new gallery. The women have their hair short like Jean Seberg and wear two-piece suits; one, a Chilean, takes the poet to task, saying poetry ought to speak to the people and that this is why she makes music; another, thin as a bulrush, is a translator. A man stands looking out the window, blond hair, skin pale, and his face triangular like that of a small fox. This is the Ukrainian, with his camera around his neck and a jealously guarded briefcase for the negatives. The people come up to Enriqueta and go away again, offering her scotch, and all of them thinking, is she one of us?

At intervals, Madame Vadim turns to a painting hanging above the oak table and cries *"Vashe zdorovie!"* At this, all present stop what they are doing and join her in the toast.

Enriqueta takes in the painting. It is an oil, a woman in profile with black hair and fulgurant eyes surrounded by snails. Enriqueta feels something she is unable to put a name to; nothing supernatural though, to be clear.

"It's by Mariette Lydis," Madame Vadim finally says.

•

Shortly afterward, Enriqueta discovers, to her horror, that she is dancing with the poet. He is telling her a story about French cutpurses, the best of which, he says, sport pretend arms crossed conspicuously at their chests, while their actual hands are behind their backs relieving you of your belongings. Enriqueta takes advantage of a momentary distraction to disentangle herself, going over and collapsing into an armchair. The Ukrainian joins her, and begins telling her about the resident ghost: a woman who steals eggs from the kitchens at night and buries them in the garden, in an attempt both to stop the rain from falling and to bring a daughter back safe and sound.

"Make yourself at home," says the translator, so thin she, too, could be an apparition. "We're picky about who we invite, but once you're in, you're family."

How did I get here? Enriqueta thinks. And then she remembers.

They met at the Argentinean Fine Arts Academy. Enriqueta and Renée were given a shared assignment to go to the lime pits and paint in the style of Correggio. They have been shown how to copy others, which is how painting is taught in art schools. And it was Enriqueta whom Renée chose, out of all the students in their year, to be her friend. She is the only one Renée views as capable of independent thought; all the rest are, to her mind, a long way down in the food chain, somewhere around the level of ants, for example.

The green aroma on the air is emanating from a bowl on the table.

"Brazilian flowers," says Renée, "you can't imagine how good. Smoke a little of that and even Brigitte Bardot would seem like interesting company."

The lips thick and full, the laughter deep; both hypnotic.

Now she begins to roll a deft joint, which she lights, inhaling deeply, and passes. Enriqueta watches how it's done and, when it comes to her, sucks hard, taking the smoke down into her lungs and then letting it out slowly. When her lungs are nearly empty, the smoke catches in her throat, sending her into a coughing fit, and again everyone is looking. They go on passing it. On her next attempt, she goes easier. Filaments of Enriqueta begin to float around the space, like a sea anemone's tentacles, spreading and then contracting, and her brain feels somehow far-flung, seems to have been deposited light-years away. Was marijuana more hallucinogenic, or purer, in those days? Something to investigate. Enriqueta perceives strange alterations in her body. She is beginning to enjoy herself, but something says not to get carried away, not to lose her footing and turn optimist. Suddenly she is seized by a desire to write down her thoughts—every one of them seems wonderfully profound. Later she will be surprised at the uniform mundanity of them.

"We've paid the rent for the month with this painting," says Renée. "The certificate of authenticity came through today."

"And Madame celebrates by blowing it all on a party?"

"That's about right."

"It's very striking."

Renée just looks at her.

"I've never seen a Lydis like this one," says Enriqueta. "It's very . . . *perfect*."

"No flies on you, Macedo."

Renée says can they speak in private. They go down a gloomy hallway, the penetrating smell of the cypresses reaching in through the windows, as though a forest had come inside the building. They arrive at the room Renée shares with the translator. On her bed, a copy of Kafka's *Amerika*, and on the translator's, a typewriter and a copy of *Clea* by Lawrence Durrell. On the floor between them, a moth-eaten tartan quilt.

PORTRAIT OF AN UNKNOWN LADY

"What are we talking about, then?" says Enriqueta, feeling suddenly uneasy.

"The Lydis. You're right, it isn't genuine."

"So where did it come from?"

"Don't play dumb."

"You did it?"

Again, that look.

"Is the certificate a forgery too?"

"The certificate is real. They handed it over this afternoon at the valuations office. It passed, can you believe?"

"Does Madame Vadim know it's a fake?"

"Madame Vadim is an open-minded person. She came through a war."

"And you're telling me this *why*?"

It was morning, but not yet light, when Lozinski walked her out to the bus stop. Enriqueta would recall the coruscating moment for years afterward: the Russian's broad back as he walked away down the sidewalk, the blur of her reflection in the bus window. She, who had always believed painting to be the product not of historical circumstance but of frustrated genius, had now been entrusted with a project.

That night at the Hotel Melancholical, Renée had

confessed that she needed someone inside the valuations department, someone she could rely on to pass her paintings as genuine. Yes, the Lydis had made it through, but what about the next one, or the ones after that? And there would be more, of course there would; the hotel residents were short of funds as always, and the idea of turning out knockoffs for quick money had been universally welcomed. Enriqueta's grade average meant she was sure to have little difficulty getting a job in the department; who could possibly suspect the golden girl? Renée, using the hotel as her base, working in the vast rooms in which the oils could dry for weeks, would take care of the rest. And this was how the Melancholical Forgers, Inc., came into being.

From the start, Renée specialized in Lydises. The Countess Govone—this being the Austrian Mariette Lydis's married name—had lived in Buenos Aires from the 1940s onward, making a name for herself with portraits of the great and the good of the city. Nowadays all families of quality—or any who wish to consider themselves as such—have a Lydis on a wall in the house. Her portraits were not always of the prettiest daughter. In fact, she was said to prefer *les jolies laides* for the kind of poetic license they allowed, never the case with your stereotypical beauties. Certain aspects recur, as though through a kind of cloning: the liquid pupils, the high cheekbones, the snub noses and wide mouths.

Lydis was a regular feature in the city's most refined circles. Porteña women liked the feeling of rubbing shoulders with a countess; a little of the prestige they so yearned for. But in time she began to withdraw, losing her taste for company. It was then that forgeries of her work began to circulate. The countess's paintings commanded decent prices, never stratospheric but remarkably consistent. The demand was always there, her work held its value well, and nobody gave too much thought to provenance. It was a style of painting that people never thought to be suspicious about, and the checks were less stringent then—today's paranoia had not yet set in.

The members of the Melancholical Forgers, Inc., had a variety of functions, but the talent resided entirely with Renée. She executed the painting, appropriating the original and making Lydis's vision her own; always, rather than "copying," she worked "in the style of" a painter, an art unto itself for the way it requires a person to enter the mind of another. It requires empathy and—why not?—a certain genius. Renée was an original forger, if such a thing can be said to exist. Once the paint was dry, in came the Ukrainian to photograph it; next the Russian, who, with his Muscovite aptitude for calligraphy, did the label on the back; the publicist, who always wore an Anselmo Spinelli coat, took the piece to a gallery; the gallery sent it for authentication; and Enriqueta, soon enrolled in the valuation department's in-house training program, saw that it was passed. It would then go back to the gallery to await a buyer, or to the auction house. It was easy, almost too easy, and there was a period in which the Melancholical Forgers, Inc., ran as regular and smooth as clockwork. Something fraternal bound them together, all making a living by cheating the rich. There was even a rumor for a time that Lydis herself, hidden away in her apartment, was in charge of the operation, and that Renée was in fact her mouthpiece in the world. It was the golden age of art forgery.

It would have been little surprise had cracks begun to appear—disputes over fair shares, power plays. The history of art is full of groups that last three years at most, but here the rule did not apply. They went on producing; what changed was the taste of the buying public. One day, the publicist took one of the Lydises to a gallery, only to be given the message "Tell Renée we can't shift these anymore."

Not a problem for a virtuoso like her. She turned her hand to the likes of Spilimbergo, Berni, and Basaldúa, and all were more than satisfactory, though they did not quite shine in the manner of her Lydises. There the transfer was seamless, entirely natural. Even Gambartes, for example, at first glance the most straightforward of artists, had his little tricks, and Renée took a cleaning job in the painter's home, sneaking into his studio at siesta time to look over his materials. Something about Renée seemed off to the lady of the house, and Señora Gambartes, looking for evidence or possibly intending to plant some, got her hands on Renée's handbag. Rather than stealing eggs or flour, the buxom domestic had been helping herself to the husband's paintbrushes.

By expanding the roster, the Melancholicals diversified their market. From a distance this would seem to have been the point of rupture, the moment at which the romantic aspect of the venture dropped away. They started accepting commissions, many of which were at the behest of a single collector—a man who is said to have claimed that Renée painted the best Figaris he owned. This, like everything else about the Melancholicals, was and remains hearsay. What is certain is that various members of the group were regular visitors to the collector's *quinta* on the outskirts of Buenos Aires, near an area of land owned by the military. It had a vast library of antique books once frequented by Borges, and a gallery with tens of Figaris and one exquisite Chagall. At the outer edge of the grounds stood a belt of contorted-looking trees, seemingly the pruning handiwork of a sadistic gardener. In summer they were in full leaf, but then winter would come and strip them, disclosing a series of steel sculptures by Enio Iommi.

Then, a gap. It seems that Renée took umbrage at learning that the painter Rodolfo Ruiz Pizarro was being paid better on account of his sex. Men create, women imitate, as the saying goes. People also said that signs of petrification were beginning to appear in Renée's work, or, in plain English, that it wasn't as good as before. But certainly a moment came when, from one day to the next, Renée's paintings stopped selling, and, very soon afterward, she disappeared. Enriqueta asked at the hotel, and was told Renée had left without giving any indication of where she'd gone. Enriqueta went on inquiring for a time after that, but nobody was able to help her.

One by one the members of the Melancholical Forgers, Inc., gave up their rooms at the hotel, which itself was sold not long afterward to an order of Swiss nuns—by which time Enriqueta had begun to be referred to at the valuations office as "Herself."

The last time their paths crossed was at the end of the 1980s, one of those winter nights when cats slide past clinging to the walls. Enriqueta was at a stoplight in the Microcentro when she saw her: limping along the pavement as though one of her high heels had snapped, pausing every now and then to peer inside bins. The lower part of her face was wrapped in a woolen scarf. Fear of catching cold? That I doubt. Self-imposed silence? Possibly. For a number of seconds, two energetic flows overlapped. The "lady" Enriqueta glimpsed was a world away from the kind who go for highlights at the hairdresser's, or inherit the family porcelain, or amass loyalty points at the supermarket. I am speaking of the creatures of the night, another class of lady altogether. The two of them looking out from their respective worlds: seeing each other but unable to make contact. Then Renée was walking past. Still that same flinty gaze. Where was this woman going? Enriqueta said to herself. Where could she be bound?

"And after that?" I said, at the end of Enriqueta's first telling of the story. "You never heard of her again?"

"I heard lots of things," Enriqueta said. "That's not to say I believed any of them."

Like King Shaka, who made his troops walk on thorns to toughen up their feet, Enriqueta's character had been formed on the basis of deceptions.

Of all the stories told to me in the sauna, it is this one that resounds most strongly in my mind. Was everything she told me true? Such details, such visions, such lifted, startling moments, cannot be made up . . . But then again, Enriqueta was the queen of making things up. I had seen with my own eyes the incredible stories she could spin about the provenance of a painting should it require "a helping hand" in the market. She needed little bidding to spin a yarn of Bruce Chatwin proportions, but from that to inventing all of this . . .

The Gallery of Illuminated Women

"After the passing of irresistible music you must make do

with a dripping faucet." So says Jim Harrison in a poem

that describes perfectly the feeling I had after Enriqueta's

death, as though the world, for me, was now a poorer

place. With her gone, I was a cow without a pasture. If I sound like the heroine in a novel, bear with me, I'll find my voice soon enough.

I resigned from the valuations office a few months later and jumped into the first thing I happened upon. I became an art critic. Not that it was of particular interest to me as a profession; in fact, when reading an art review I tended to scan the first five or six lines, skip to the last two or three, and end up thinking, what's with these people? Traumatic childhoods? But working with Enriqueta had been a training for my eye, and suddenly criticism seemed like an easy option. I soon got a job at a daily newspaper. Nobody's out there killing themselves for a job on an arts desk, and that should have been my clue: if there's something nobody wants, there must be a reason.

I was given the job of covering the minor openings; it had been years since the senior critic could bring herself to show any interest in these—a woman who would merit a chapter of her own, but I can sum her up in a few lines, invoking Félix Fénéon: "She tended to go where there was wine on offer, a drink you never get at any show worth its salt. Her kleptomania was also remarkable. She stole only objects that were difficult to hide: a serving platter, a lamp, a punch bowl."

I liked her, that's probably obvious. I soon realized that writing about art is a relatively simple thing once one gets the knack. You see the object, you translate this vision into words and add any speculation you deem relevant. If no vision comes, the artwork can also be written about using words that are not your own, other people's words artfully reassembled. I wasn't fooling myself: reviews of the visual arts were the most neglected strand in all the supplements, meaning you could get away with writing whatever you liked.

She got the bylines for all my early reviews, but being neither mean nor unworldly-wise, she soon let me start publishing under my own name. To have one's name in print is a high-impact weapon. Before long people started to look out for my reviews; I was giving thumbs-ups and thumbs-downs, and while I won't say I was changing the course of art history, I did have a certain amount of sway. This was toward the end of any influence being exerted by critics; now it is curators who call all the shots.

I watched the art-world episodes in Perry Mason's TV show and would every so often rent *Laura*, the film in which the art critic character, Waldo Lydecker, writes up his notes in the bath, destroying reputations with the saber slashes of his pen. I believe I personally kept the video store on the corner in business through the end of that century. But there were nights when I intentionally decided not to turn the television on, and in its place, Enriqueta would appear in my dreams. We'd be walking through an empty gallery, no pictures anywhere, no sculptures, and she would dole out aphorisms like a wise queen, but there was no boastfulness in them; it was only her liking for brevity that made her talk like this.

These dreams became the best thing in my life. I would wake to a calm, clean existence. There were days when I didn't think I was going to be able to stand it; I wept with boredom. How monstrous the past, especially if it happens to have been heady. How I missed those days. But in the same way that Bach asked people not to let him go out armed in the streets in case he felt a sudden urge to kill, I kept away from temptations. If some recent case of art fraud should come up around the water cooler, I'd act uninterested. I'd look at the lapacho trees flowering bright pink outside the window, while in reality viewing things hidden deep within me.

Sometimes the monotony would be interrupted, and that was wonderful. I was the only person left in the office one day when I looked up and saw an old man in a green frock coat approaching me. He walked as though along a cliff edge, seemingly about to topple into the abyss but always, at the last moment, stepping back from the brink. His boots were cherry pink and polished to a shine. At a stretch, one could have struck a match with those boots.

I knew immediately who it was: Lozinski. Time had not treated him well, I thought—as if I myself were unscathed.

"We meet again," I said, keeping my cool, as though it were the most normal thing in the world for ghosts to step into my path. "All well?"

"Just as you see, Señorita M. Growing old gracefully." His grammar as ever faultless—to a fault.

I offered the Russian some nuts in a bowl. I had lately been keeping nuts to hand at all times, in imitation of Rachmaninov, who always had pistachios within easy reach as a way of keeping his fears at bay. Lozinski sat down facing me.

The first thing we talked about was not the weather but the past, which is another way of talking about the weather. Lozinski told me how good life under the tsars had been and about his father going to see Lenin at the Smolny Palace in 1918 to ask for work, though Lozinski never found out what kind.

"Speaking of work," he said, "I've got something for you."

"One last roll of the dice, then, Lozinski?"

I knew of Matilde only from descriptions, but her appearance was as familiar to me as that of a lifelong friend. She had been Renée's roommate at the Hotel Melancholical and was so thin she reminded people of a chick fallen from the nest before fledging. She would sit on the bed, legs crossed, her Olivetti and her carbon paper always near to hand, and read the French surrealist poets. Matilde liked painting—as a descendant of Chagall it was in her blood— but she spoke English rather than Russian. Cortázar had been one of her students and she had worked as an in-house translator, a great one in an era of great translations, for the Sudamericana publishing house. When something other than night darkened the streets of Buenos Aires she moved to Barcelona to translate Tolkien. She and Lozinski still corresponded; he was the only habitué of the Hotel Melancholical with whom she had stayed in touch. "They tell me the translation turned out beautifully, very poetic, though I never saw poetry in Tolkien. I must have read all that when I was younger; at my age I've seen a bit, and there's so much that doesn't seem authentic to me now." She was living in Ibiza by this point, in the old people's home on Cas Serres, and more or less in penury.

"I don't know who there can be for her to talk to," said Lozinski, helping himself to the last nut in the bowl. "Most of the old people on Ibiza speak the Balearic dialect. To her it must sound like the clucking of a chicken."

"Why are you here, Lozinski?"

The Russian smiled. He opened a packet of Lucky

Strikes, took a lighter from his inside pocket, and rolled his thumb over the flint so that a flame leaped up.

"That's precisely what I'm trying to tell you, Señorita M . . ."

Again he paused. He dropped his head, like a toy rabbit with the cord removed. But his internal workings weren't broken. He was looking for something.

I don't know where he'd been hiding it; I hadn't noticed it when he came in. He lifted it onto the table with some effort and pushed it toward me. Nobody had opened the leather satchel for a long time and the brass clasp was rusty. I took a Swiss Army knife out of a drawer and eased it into the lock, which opened eventually. The first thing I saw was a bundle of letters neatly tied with kitchen string, and next to that a bundle of postcards; beneath these were some lithographs with sheets of waxed paper as dividers and then some books and newspaper cuttings. There was more, but the detail isn't the point; the basic idea was already forming in my mind.

"What is all this?" I asked, though I barely needed to.

"Memorabilia . . . things that once belonged to—well, you can see who."

"Yes, I can read. Mariette Lydis. Originals?"

"As far as I know."

"And how did you come across them?"

Then followed the most words in a sequence I'd probably ever heard from him:

"Madame Vadim left everything to me, and I've got
the Lydis that was in the Hotel Melancholical. It's gathering dust back in my hostel. I've got these things too, all
of which Madame acquired over the years, following the
advice of her grandfather Dmitri, who was the curator at
the Kiev museum and had taught her that a painting is
worth more if there's a story behind it. When Lydis died,
Madame started gathering all her things together. She became friendly with the doorman in the building where
the countess had lived, went through the bags that were
sent to Cotolengo after her death. She trawled the flea
markets—thirty years ago, you could still find the most
incredible things in those places. Sadly for Madame, she
didn't see her plan come to fruition, but she left me in-
structions. Lydis's star would rise again—I just needed to
keep a weather eye out. Then, a few weeks ago, I was on
my balcony watching the sunset when an idea came to
me: maybe the time's come, I said to myself. The owl of
Minerva doesn't go out hunting till twilight—"

"Where's this all heading?" I said, cutting him off.

Really, I knew the answer. It's rare for a man to suggest something to a woman without her, minutes earlier,
having already guessed what it is.

The Russian smiled—he still had a lot of faith in the power of that faded smile.

"I've got the good looks," he said, "you've got the brains, my friend Matilde needs the cash . . . We're a trio made in heaven, don't you think?"

"Clearly, Lozinski, clearly."

So we found ourselves face-to-face in a moral desert, with no shade to protect us and no fresh water either. The picture from the Hotel Melancholical had sought me out, not the other way around; in reality, I'd done nothing, which as an approach to life isn't without its problems but at the same time isn't a crime. It felt as though they were Enriqueta's threads, being tugged on from some unknown place. The plan took clear shape before my eyes: an artist with a past, a collector with a future. It was a union we had to make happen. We would set up an auction of Lydis-related work.

It was at this point that I ought to have stopped, thanked the Russian for coming to me, and seen him to the door. But I didn't. Instead, I said yes to the proffered Lucky Strike.

•

55

Let us go back to what we know.

Had I actually thought it through? I believe I must have, at some point between the evening of the Russian's appearance and the next morning, which was when I picked up the phone and called my contact at the auction house.

"It's a great chance to do a good thing," I said to Alfonso, while running the fork across my tongue a little more slowly than usual. I think Alfonso was involved in an imaginary conversation with some other person because he answered by saying, "The reason I have a mustache is to smell my previous night's misdemeanors."

He placed his hand on mine. Alfonso is the kind who thinks that if a person spends their life not falling in love with anybody, then everyone will love them. Perhaps he's right.

I went bright red, that mischievous color that is not our fault but the blood's entirely; it is the blood, after all, that leaps impetuously out from the heart. When I said the words "Mariette Lydis" and "auction," it was as though Alfonso suddenly seemed to step off his hurtling erotic toboggan, as he abruptly took his hand from mine. Not that it did anything to check the mounting sparkle in his eye. His attentiveness was not out of courtesy, but because he already had a buyer in mind. I gave myself an inner pat on the back; I'd gone to the right person. Alfonso didn't even mention the possibility of the goods being of less than distinguished provenance, though he did ask that there not be any gaps. I couldn't help but feel slightly impressed by the implacable, almost French cynicism my friend displayed.

He asked me back to his to continue the discussion in private and, a couple of Johnnie Walkers later, we felt inspired enough to start thinking about the detail. We considered the plan from all angles.

"Won't people realize?" I said in a moment of alcohol-induced weakness.

"Realize what?"

"Oh, I don't know. Aren't collectors obsessed with the possibility of forgeries?"

The look Alfonso shot me seemed to say, forgeries? Even the museums are stuffed with works once thought authentic that later, when the error was spotted, stayed in situ on the basis of their quality.

I put my doubts to one side. We eventually spelled out the particulars of our arrangement, the projected modus operandi. The idea was for me to do the research but, to avoid raising suspicions, for him to present the whole thing as his own doing—a very common approach among auction-house staff. "Bringing back the dead," they call it when a forgotten artist is rediscovered, and those steering proceedings are known as "Resurrection men." I came away from that meeting with such a sense of purpose. Oh, to think of the guts I had then! How different I must have been.

I've heard it said that "opportunity" is another word for "temptation." I spent the ensuing days adjusting to the idea of what I was intending, so that, by training my gaze on it like this, it ended up seeming a thing worthy of praise.

Operation Lydis would mean rescuing an artist before the muddy tide of events washed her away forever, with the entirety of the money going to help a sweet, elderly translator in her Balearic dotage. The mission was simple and not without a touch of nobility, but my hands shook as though the Devil himself had taken hold of them. I know his fame as an adversary who flees at the first sign of resistance, but I was tired of the fight. On top of that, aren't our weak points lovelier than our strengths? I set about reading everything I could find on Lydis, and then sat down at my desk to put the catalogue together. I was thorough, because living outside the law takes honesty. So Bob Dylan said in one of his songs, having himself taken the line from Don Siegel's *The Lineup*. It's like this: all of humanity, in the final reckoning, is a single book, one that it's possible to take scissors and glue to in order to create one's own report, which in a way is what I did. I wrote through the night and when I had finished, in imitation of my former mentor in the good days, blew across the tip of my index finger.

AUCTION CATALOGUE:
POSSESSIONS OF MARIETTE LYDIS

Included: postcards, paperweights & works in gouache
belonging to the artist
April 7, 1997, 14:30
SÁNCHEZ DÁVILA REMATES

Lot 1

Postcard of *Highland Princess*

Suggested starting price: US$500

In June 1914, shortly before the outbreak of the First
World War, five students from the Royal Academy of

Arts boarded a train for Bristol. The British navy was due to try a new camouflage technique known as "razzle dazzle." The man behind the idea, artist and fisherman Norman Wilkinson, had put his hypothesis to the high command: not even the latest U-boat, he explained, would be able to judge the distance to its target if faced with an assemblage of maniacal stripes. The key was to produce an optical vibration that would render the British ships *ultra*-visible; visible to the point of being dazzling. His speech was met with approval and a number of days later in the port of Bristol sixty ships were placed under canvas on scaffolds for the Royal Academicians to paint with geometric stripes—black and white, or red and green, or yellow and black. It was the kind of constructivist experiment that in later years, when the captains of the German U-boats returned home and told of their encounters with these underwater trompe l'œils, the Bauhaus would later encourage its students to undertake. In military terms the razzle-dazzle technique was neither a failure nor a success, but force of habit saw its use continue through to the Second World War. As she was being readied to set sail, the *Highland Princess* resembled a freshly painted Easter egg, or a zebra in the water.

Lot 2
Pigskin valise
Suggested starting price: US$2,000

Two hundred and fifty passengers step on board, among
them forty unaccompanied minors who skip up the gang-
plank as though passing through the entrance to an amuse-
ment park. Countess Mariette Lydis Govone, like all good
Viennese, has no interest in children, all of her affection
being taken up by her pet poodle; loose tongues suggest
she uses it as a masturbation aid. The small dog travels in its
basket alongside the pigskin valises with M.L.G. stamped
on the sides. A herd of Yorkshire swine must have gone
into the making of this luggage set. Gripping the railing,
the polish from which leaves marks on her gloves, the
countess watches as they leave the coast behind. Her gaze
is distant, but there is nothing romantic about it.

Lot 3
Sketch of Countess Castiglione on board *Highland Princess*
Suggested starting price: US$3,000

They say travel leads to the realization that one does not in
fact exist. Two days later, the *Highland Princess* is sailing with
all its windows boarded up as enemy aircraft fly overhead.
There is the intermittent sound of missiles whistling through

the air, though never that of the explosions. Mariette Lydis takes out sketchbook and pencils from time to time; she has only to glance at a scene to take in everything she needs from it. She sees long-legged English, scruffy Americans, portly Germans. An Italian woman catches her eye: she speaks in Tuscan with her husband and in German with her female companion, selecting languages as though choosing among petit fours. When she asks Lydis, in French, if she is an artist, Lydis responds, "I dabble," and shows her some pictures. Her false humility: a way of winning praise. Alone in the cabin, for it is only *à deux* that women know how to be friends, Lydis draws her. The woman is altogether biddable; the art of posing for pictures is an Italian trait through and through. There are immobile days under the sun when it is so quiet that not even the sea can be heard. And days when the wind whips them and the ship pitches about terribly and it is more a case of clambering amidships than walking. The helmsman explains to the countess that the rocking is because of badly stowed coal below. And, putting on airs, he gestures at a green-black line on the far horizon.

"The coast at last?" she asks.

"No," he says, "sharks."

Lot 4
Dried birch branch
Suggested starting price: US$25

Baden bei Wien is the oldest spa town in Austria. The Romans named it Thermae Pannonicae for its sulfurous mineral waters, which remain constantly between 33°C and 37°C and are effective in healing rheumatism and gout. On a visit with his wife, Mozart composed the *Ave verum corpus*. Beethoven went there, hoping to cure his hearing problems, but the steam only aggravated the problem and he ended up having to wear earplugs. A common fin de siècle sight was that of people in white towels and dressing gowns walking the town's heated galleries carrying birch branches. Baden bei Wien was the birthplace of Marietta Ronsperger, later known as Mariette Lydis, and later still as Countess Govone.

Lot 5
Pearl necklace
Suggested starting price: US$25,000
The smell of the sulfurous waters drifted to young Marietta's window from the Hohenstaufenstrasse. She had a father with a talent for tricking women who deployed this skill in selling them pearls, which was a profitable trade before the invention of artificial pearls. She had a strict teacher for a mother. Her older brother had a lazy eye, and, at a loss for what to do, they went for advice to one Dr. Krantz, who had published a notable study on the subject in two volumes. But the doctor was unable to give a

clear diagnosis. The mother left the house very early one morning with the boy, and with Mariette looking on from her window; she saw them cross the Augarten. When the mother came back it was dark and she was on her own.

Lot 6
Tagesblatt, dated November 23, 1888
Suggested starting price: US$500

The morning edition of the *Tagesblatt* brings the news from the capital. In Vienna's Burgtheater the painting of *The Cart of Thespis* on the staircase ceiling panels is complete, the work of one Gustav Klimt, who, it appears, is not pleased with the job; he is trapped in an old world when what he wants to do is explore the new. He tries to slip a depiction of two women kissing into one of the preliminary sketches, but the man in charge of the theater's redecoration, Baron Von Wilbrandt, steps in. In other news: the gas streetlamps in Vienna have been replaced by electric ones and it has become a common sight to see young people giving themselves electric shocks in Prater Park; in their fascination with all things modern, many of them end up in the hospital. Prince Rodolfo is encouraging people to begin using telephones, but the Viennese see these new contraptions as nothing but a rococo bubble: calls are limited to ten minutes, of which six are lost in the arabesques of protocol. "Fräulein operator in Baden?" says Fräulein operator in Vienna. "May I have the honor of wishing you a good day? It is my privilege to be able to connect you with His Excellency, Baron Von W., who wishes personally to extend his complements to His Excellency . . . Of course, His Excellency would be most grateful for the opportunity to count on the enormous pleasure of conversing . . ." In Austria, progress makes no sense to anyone.

Lot 7
Photograph: Sissi mounting Nihilist
Suggested starting price: US$800

Even the Danube is turbid at the end of the nineteenth century; cases of typhus have been reported among several families. Marietta travels reluctantly to Persia, Greece, Milan, Morocco, and Switzerland. If it were up to her, she would travel in her mind. Her companion is the cousin of Fanny Angerer, the celebrated hairdresser who earns more at the court of Vienna seeing to Empress Sissi's coiffure than a tenured university professor, and her stories are trips in themselves . . . In honor of the tradition of young truants, Empress Sissi flees Vienna. In her new home on Madeira she rides Nihilist, her favorite Arab horse, and though her hair is ankle-length she prefers to wear it up, thick plaits coiled about her head, the weight of which gives her terrible cervical pain. She eats nothing but ice cubes and chunks of white bread, wears a damp bodice, which as it dries tightens even more about the waist, straps slabs of beef around her legs at night to tone the skin, and, when she turns thirty-five, the age at which women begin to dry out, conceals her face behind a leather fan. "I will cover myself forever," she says, "that death may be left to work alone, in quiet, upon my skin." Melodrama, yes, but the better sort. At this point young Marietta urges the storyteller along, eager to hear about the more recent years, including the renowned gallery of beautiful women. It was during a stay in Venice that the empress started collecting photographs from across Europe. She wrote to her brother-in-law, Archduke Louis Victor, saying, "I have begun an album and am collecting photographs of women. I would appreciate you sending me all the beautiful faces you meet." Marietta wants to have a gallery of beautiful women as well, but her idea is to paint them. She dreams of being an artist, but her parents are against the idea, not knowing that their opposition provides their daughter with the gift of necessity.

Lot 8
Letters between Lydis and Bontempelli
Suggested starting price: US$1,200

In a few short years, the myth of happy Vienna gave way to that of neurotic Vienna, and because women tend to find practical solutions to their worries, Marietta departed the city in 1915 on the arm of the Greek millionaire playboy

Jean Lydis, who turned her into Mariette Lydis and took her to live in Athens, in a faded pink villa by the sea. Every morning at breakfast, he hid emeralds among her grapes. It was like paradise, but she wasn't made to live in paradise. "The moment I saw you I felt the lions prowling inside me," Mariette wrote to Massimo Bontempelli, the dusky-haired Italian poet who appeared at the villa one day. Seeing in her a creature of the same species, Bontempelli invited her to Paris.

Lot 9

Charcoal sketches with oriental influence

Suggested starting price: US$1,500

She was beautiful, yes, but had her lips been fleshier, she would have been perfection. She was still sufficiently attractive to suck the air out of any room she entered. Her blond hair, the way it seemed lit from within, was impossible to ignore, which went for her eyes as well, the gray of seabirds, and her air of unease. In Paris, Mariette Lydis began showing her paintings. There was a marked oriental influence in her pictures; it is probable that her trips to Persia in adolescence had fired the sensuousness of her imagination.

Lot 10

Les Fleurs du Mal by Charles Baudelaire. Paris, G. Govone 1928. Color illustrations by Mariette Lydis. No.

115 in print run of 290 on Hollande Pannekoek paper.
Suggested starting price: US$2,500
She met Govone, editor of Les Presses de l'Hôtel de Sa-
gonne, at an evening party on the Rive Gauche. *Les Fleurs
du Mal* was the first thing she illustrated for him. Thanks
to the scrupulousness of the French when it comes to
conserving written artefacts, we have a page torn from
a notebook in which Govone writes of the pair's "strong
and unreasonable passion" for one another (*Chers papiers*,
Lot, Seghers, 1991). The Austrian Mariette Lydis went on
to become Countess Govone.

Lot 11
Series of flower paintings in aquarelle
Suggested starting price: US$5,500
Lydis's Asiatic concerns were supplanted in a period when
she began producing images of murderous little girls and
saints, floral profusions reminiscent of the work of the
Dutch painter Rachel Ruysch, as well as strange animal
mutations—shapes morphing into rabbits, parrots, lizards,
and swans—and, later, or at the same time, a Hogarthian
phase with depictions of prostitutes and criminals, which
prompted a critic to call her "a Botticelli in the world of
Dostoyevsky."

Lot 12

Portrait of unknown woman, oil, c. 1920

Suggested starting price: US$1,000

"*Marqué par la rêverie fatale,*" say the critics when discussing the strange eyes of the subjects in her portraits. Among the French there are those who exalt her work, while others consider her a witch. An intimate of de Montherlant, she spends nights on the Quai Voltaire in a fortress overlooking the river so synonymous with that writer.

Lot 13

Photograph of Lydis with Kisling and Foujita, c. 1920

Suggested starting price: US$1,500

The countess had eye shadow made of kohl, the oriental powder fashionable at the time after its sanctification by Colette in her short tract on makeup: "If you bathe in the sun by day, and by night in artificial light, use kohl, even at night." Lydis spent her free evenings drifting through the dives of Paris. At her favorite bistro, Chez Palmyre, she took private French lessons, diabolically private, with Palmyre himself, and also met Moïse Kisling, Foujita, and Count Lascano Tegui. It was this latter personage who first mentioned Buenos Aires to her.

Lot 14

Amelia Earhart's flying jacket, property of Lydis

Suggested starting price: US$55,000

She was working on plans to circumnavigate the globe in her Lockheed Electra. It was the one remaining passage she had left to do. Amelia Earhart took smelling salts with her to avoid falling asleep, since she drank neither coffee nor tea. She also took a hairbrush along, wanting to be presentable for the cameras when she landed. But on July 2, 1937, the plane made its last contact with the cutter *Itasca*, which was acting as picket ship: "We must be on you, but we cannot see you. Fuel is running low." A number of hours later, there was no sign of the aircraft. "Search under way for Amelia in the vicinity of Howland Island," *Le Poste Parisien* repeated for hours. Before boarding that flight, Earhart had left Lydis with some old flying equipment: a jacket, goggles, cap. All the garments were grease-stained. "Why do you fly?" Lydis asked her the night before she set off. "To get away from myself," said Earhart.

Lot 15

***The Fanfarlo, and Other Verse* by Muriel Spark (Hand and Flower Press: Ashford, Kent, 1952)**

Suggested starting price: US$1,100

The Nazis are meters short of the French border. Alongside Erica Marx, the countess flees to Winchcombe, an

English town in the Cotswolds. Erica is Karl Marx's grand-daughter and works at Count Govone's press. The women rent a house together on Hailes Street, to the right of the greengrocer's and across the street from the butcher's, and as a way to pass the time set up the Hand and Flower Press, a publisher specializing in unknown poets, including Muriel Spark. Lydis spends the later parts of the day practicing putting on gas masks.

"I am trying to get used to the blackout," she writes in a letter to Count Govone, who has gone to Italy. But the war is affecting her nerves. One day she books passage on board the *Highland Princess*. It is the last boat to leave England.

Lot 16

Duncan Haws, *Merchant Fleets in Profile*, Vol. 5 (Patrick Stephen Ltd., 1978), 160pp
First edition, hardcover
Suggested starting price: US$150
From the port in Buenos Aires, Mariette Lydis takes her final look at the *Highland Princess*. A pair of tugboats tows it out to sea, they pass one buoy, two, three, and as the steel cables disengage, the liner's propeller kicks in. Two years later—in spite of its razzle-dazzle design—it will be hit by a torpedo in the port of Liverpool. Later still, it will be bought by the Greek impresario and magnate-to-be John Latsis, and in contravention of seafaring tradition,

according to which it is bad luck to change a vessel's name, the new owner rechristens it. Of all the possible names, he chooses *Marietta*. Its eventual fate is not entirely clear, but according to Duncan Haws's *Merchant Fleets in Profile,* Vol. 5, the *Marietta* is hit by a Morska mine in Singapore and grounded in the port, where methadone addicts will make a home of it. It will end its days near Chittagong, in a ghostly cemetery on the coast of Bangladesh where vessels are scrapped in order to be turned into metal sheeting.

Lot 17

Collection of Baccarat paperweights

Suggested starting price: US$15,000

Europe slid off her like the shed skin of a reptile. The possibilities of her adopted land are immediately clear to her. In Buenos Aires she installs herself for a time in a suite at the Hotel Plaza, before moving into the apartment she will inhabit for the rest of her life at 1278 Calle Cerrito, between Juncal and Arenales. For a time she can sleep only for short snatches; the sea is still in motion inside her. It is also suffocatingly hot, and her first winter spent outside Europe is marked by the count sending her eighteen Baccarat paperweights so that she may feel the cool of their glass surfaces in her hands.

Lot 18

Copy of *Escape from Anger*, Robert Manfred (Erica Marx's pen name) (Hand and Flower Press: Aldington, Kent, 1951)

Suggested starting price: US$2,200

Erica Marx sends word from Kent: the secret services are keeping tabs on her cottage because she has taken in Una Wing, the prostitute who married John Amery, the scion of a wealthy family who collaborated with Hitler and will end up being hanged. "The most polite traitor I ever met," said Erica Marx. At the end of the war, she sells the press and moves into a houseboat on the Thames where she begins research into dowsing, paraphysics, and sonic therapies. During this period she writes an article entitled "Do Humans Have a Compass in Their Nose?" discussing a minute crystal of magnetite located between the eyes, directly behind the nose, the same kind of crystal as is found in homing pigeons, migrating salmon, and great white sharks. It functions like a compass that follows the magnetic fields of the earth and is what enables us to orientate ourselves. She returns to Winchcombe occasionally with a small, Y-shaped branch, walking the paths there in search of magnetic flows. It is likely that she misses Mariette and that all of the above is included in the category of "things one does so as not to lose one's way."

Lot 19

Nocturne, lithograph, 1939

Suggested starting price: US$8,000

The art dealer Federico Müller offers Lydis her first Buenos Aires exhibition. In his gallery on Calle Florida, she spreads out her drawings, oil paintings, engravings, and lithographs. Her old friend de Montherlant is quoted in the catalogue as saying, "Truly great is the artist who can be man and woman at the same time! Mariette Lydis is such an artist."

Lot 20

Drawing, *Enfant des bois*, 1944

Suggested starting price: US$12,200

Lydis had to call on all of her artistic guile to transform the disadvantages of her exile into a trump card. She consolidated her style in Buenos Aires. In the portraits, men were all but nonexistent; it is women who occupy the stage, certain common denominators binding them together: the lips full and a little evil-looking, the liquid pupils and luminous irises. The swollen mouths anticipate the rash of Botox use in the city fifty years later; the raccoon eyes prefigure those of Daryl Hannah in *Blade Runner*; the neon effect, those inner-lit eyes, will be seen again in *Children of the Corn*, from Stephen King's short story. They resemble women about to turn into animals, or animals not long since made human. The aesthetic of her paintings in these years has the sad, slightly sickly sheen of the goldfish Louis XV had imported from China to entertain Madame de Pompadour.

Lot 21

Portrait, *Soucis et plaisir de Cynthia*, oil on canvas, 1951
Suggested starting price: US$3,200

Lydis's studio is on the far side of a terrace that resembles a hanging garden. Her students are the daughters of well-to-do Buenos Aires ladies. A model who posed for her sixty years ago, and who asked to remain anonymous, said, "My mother would drop me off and come back to pick me up two hours later. While I was modeling, the countess asked if I wanted ice cream; she'd ring a glass bell and a secretary called Ye would come in—she always wore a man's suit and tie; I was frightened of her. There was one girl, Maria Karen, a student whose pictures were exactly like Lydis's, which infuriated her. When it was time for me to be picked up, Lydis would say, 'This girl is my creation,' and that made my mother's hairs stand on end. And we did look alike. She invited me to go to the country with her at one point, but I wasn't allowed. Another time we traveled to Venice and saw an exhibition of hers, because my portrait was in it. This would have been around 1952. The gallery was on the Grand Canal and there were something like thirty portraits altogether, all of them of girls, and all bearing a slight resemblance to her. She gave me these very fleshy lips. They looked so absurd that when we got the painting back to Buenos Aires and hung it in the house, Mama got her oil paints out and tried to make the lips thinner. It ended up looking even stranger than it had before."

Lot 22

Notes found in the drawer of Lydis's bedroom

Suggested starting price: US$1,500

"GABRIELLE: half Arab, half French. She is a painter, models to get the money to pay for classes. Intelligent, serious. Married."

"OLGA: petite, languid eyes, hair cut *à la garçonne*. Suffers from neurasthenia and spends hours staring in the mirror. Wants to be friends. Have warned her I'm slow to make friends. Said she'd heard I like women—who doesn't? I said. Goodbye, *mademoiselle*, I said when she left—she looked at me and, serious, said, call me Olga."

"RENÉE: dark skin, full lips. After she left, I waited for her to call. Thought, telephone, O little black god, ring or I shall strangle you here and now."

Lot 23

Drawing, *Étude de petite fille aliénée*, 1940

Suggested starting price: US$1,500

Found in one of Lydis's appointment books, in her handwriting: "The asylum: in Athens, Paris, Milan, Greece,

Morocco, in Buenos Aires, the same revolting smell in all the mental hospitals of the world. The only difference is the number of flies, though their presence seems inevitable. The color white predominates; it gives a feeling of the medieval. The women, whose hair is always disheveled, come in two categories: those with eyes that sparkle, those with eyes that are dead. Their voices sound metallic, as though they were inside a watering can. They pee where they stand—on their feet—like horses."

Lot 24
Risqué engravings attributed to Lydis
Suggested starting price: US$1,500
"There is something in me as unstable as water," Lydis wrote in her notebook. At the flower boutique in one corner of the Hotel Plaza, where books in English and French were sold, and engravings and flower arrangements made by the owner, Julia Bullrich de Saint—a close friend of Lydis's—while tea and scones were being served, one could also buy risqué images including the more accessible erotic pictures made by Lydis and Suzanne Ballivet; for a different price there were *shunga* by Utamaro and Hokusai.

Lot 25
Portrait, *A Woman Passed By*, oil on canvas, 1963
Suggested starting price: US$33,300

When she turned seventy, Lydis made as much of a fuss as Queen Elizabeth: old age had crept up on her. In the years immediately before, she had set up her own gallery of illuminated women: portraits possessed of an artificial luminosity, variations on the theme of the shining nymph. The light these women give off is neither blessed nor malign; rather it is an esoteric light, the legendary astral light present in theosophical thinking from Madame Blavatsky through to Rudolf Steiner.

Lot 26
Portrait of an unknown lady, oil on canvas, c. 1960
Suggested starting price: US$33,300
The last lover she kept in her life, thirty years her junior, announced that she was going away. Lydis painted her with snails all around her; it was not simply among her last paintings, but the very last. "On your return, the mirror will tell me if I can see you," the countess wrote to her. "But will you still be young enough?"

Lydis died on April 26, 1970. The map at the Recoleta Cemetery tells us her body lies in niche 212. But this information is out of date. Niche 212 was sold off years ago. Lydis exists only in her pictures and paintings.

My Life as Critic

There's so much that can possibly go badly that it's almost

a miracle when something goes well. Operation Lydis was

a success; all of the lots were acquired by a single buyer, an

industrial engineer called Correa for whom the Viennese

Mariette Lydis represented "the final years of yesterday's world." Correa was a peculiar case, a man who bought art neither for social affirmation nor as a safe investment, and who wasn't even interested in future profitability: he bought art for the love of it, a volatile approach that no algorithm can possibly account for.

But it's not for me to judge. The important part was that following the auction Lozinski traveled to Ibiza, a fanny pack under his green frock coat and in it a lot of money for the elderly translator, his friend from the Hotel Melancholical days.

So Operation Lydis was done, but there was something that hadn't gone into the catalogue. A book with faded gold, mildew-speckled covers. In vertical, Chinese-calligraphy-like lettering, the front cover read *Der Mantel der Träume (The Cloak of Dreams)*.

This book is far and away my favorite work containing illustrations by Lydis, one that came about through an unexpected planetary conjunction when, in the autumn of 1922, the Viennese social reformer Eugenie Schwarzwald went to Béla Balázs, a Hungarian émigré, with a proposal: one of her young wards had completed a series of aquarelles and was looking for someone to base a short story collection around them. Young Balázs was part of a group of émigrés in Vienna and a coming literary man; Béla Lugosi, Robert Musil, and Arthur Schnitzler would come and drink coffee at his table. Balázs wrote operas, novels, poetry, plays, film scripts, political articles, and film reviews, and had worked on a movie with Pabst, Eisenstein, and Leni Riefenstahl, until the latter read *Mein Kampf* and removed him from the credits for being a Jew. He was a versatile man, Balázs, the quintessential modern man, the kind who knew everyone and turned his hand to everything, all genres of writing included. In a matter of three weeks—the publisher, D. R. Bischoff, stipulated that the short story collection had to be in bookshops before Christmas—he wrote *Der Mantel der Träume*, all of the stories in which were inspired by Lydis's aquarelles. Balázs's fables of terror are strange things, but most disquieting about the book are the images contained in it, which have the capacity to touch, like an acupuncture needle, a neuralgic point inside my brain. They are miles apart from the kitsch portraits for which Lydis would later be recognized, though they clearly anticipated the instability that was to pursue the countess for the rest of her days. A group of fat, unctuous men sitting at the bathhouse; a haggard, two-headed emperor; an exhausted old man surrounded by the skulls of his ancestors: they are dreams that oscillate among Aubrey Beardsley's modernist grotesque, Soutine's expressionism, and that which at the beginning of the 1900s was known as German *chinoiserie*. There is something of the caricature to the aquarelles, but a kind of very serious caricature, verging on blasphemy. They are images capable of feeding whole weeks of fantasy and speculation. How did the young Mariette happen upon the emotional wavelength necessary for registering such scenes?

I borrowed this book from Lozinski's valise and have taken it with me everywhere I've gone since then; in fact, I have it here at the hotel, in the wardrobe safe. To think of this object produces an involuntary twitch at the edge of my mouth. It is the physiognomy of the tiger savoring the pleasure of a good night's dinner.

Even a child of five knows that all happiness brings a shadow after it. It's happened to me so many times that I find it impossible to accept a gift from the gods without, one second later, turning my thoughts to the string of future troubles with which I'll have to pay for my good luck. And so in the same way that nothing in my world stood still, following the high of the auction, my spirits took on pendular motion. It began to feel as though my equalizer was out, my internal dimmer switch broken. To add another image to the pile, here's the right one: I was sitting in a hammock that swung back and forth and did not touch the ground once. I never was more slapdash with the periods and commas in my articles than during those days of supine worry.

On the one hand, I entered a comatose state. Nothing to do. Or rather, the same old routine, which was like having nothing to do. Attend third-rate exhibitions, drink cheap wine, smile, feign enthusiasm, promise to go to workshops that will never take place, say over and over, how wonderful, how interesting, all the usual art-world patter, go home, down a glass of water to dilute the wine, sit at computer, get supposedly engaged review down, the succession of hackneyed phrases, "the work is in dialogue with its environment"; "the installation interrogates the space-time continuum"; "the video poses radical questions of our everyday perception." Language of the shyster, empty language, language just to occupy column inches. Then finish up with some rhapsodic flourish and hit send before forgetting what was actually in the exhibition. There were sometimes two, three in a week, there was no need to go to them all. The photographs gave a fairly good idea.

My apathy would give way to manic effervescence. I developed the habit, to put it one way, of seeing Enriqueta at openings. It wasn't St. Francis seeing visions at Laverna. I wasn't even seeing dead people—what I was seeing was a double, which, being more real, was also the more hair-raising. The first time was with an old lady at an exhibition on Calle Arroyo. She looked exactly the same as Enriqueta from behind, even down to the way she was leaning in very close to look at the painting, as though to get light-headed on the turpentine. It quite literally bowled me over: I hit the floor, and found myself unable to move for several moments, couldn't see, but I heard people cry out, footsteps coming closer, and a voice that said, "I always did think she was rather strange." I got to my feet, keeping my composure, and asked for a glass of water.

The second time I saw Enriqueta's double was at a hip young gallery near the Atlanta Courts in Villa Crespo. Much as she was trying to fit in with her Quilmes beer in hand, the old woman could not help but stand out in that crowd of beards and tight T-shirts. I don't know if it was the same woman as before or someone else; the fact is they were the same woman! It put me in such a state, I ended up at a first-aid station. All clear on the ECG. The doctor told me it was a sinusoidal tachycardia: "You've got a good heart," she said. Me, a good heart? I didn't have it in me to set her straight.

It was then that I asked for some time off. Strangely, nobody protested. I was living alone at the time, a state that felt more and more natural. I shut myself in my apartment for several weeks, living the life of an anchorite, and it wasn't as if I had been particularly sociable before. I read occult-science journals, watched hours of television, especially Sister Wendy Beckett's art program, and would only go out at night when hunger pangs forced me, a desire I easily placated, or fooled, with an overcooked hot dog or two from the stall on the corner, these resembling more than anything keloid scars. I'd walk around the block to help the food go down and hurry home to peel an orange with my Swiss Army knife for dessert; I wanted to be there in case fate should come knocking at my door. My confused mind did settle down, and I was able to go back over the encounters with Enriqueta's double with my thoughts in less of a muddle. Proust said that the variability of appearance of human beings is strictly limited, so much so that it doesn't matter where we are, the pleasure of running into someone we think we know will always be available to us. For every single person, there are seven replicas. This struck me as explanation enough, and with it, the door blown open by such strong currents now slammed shut.

Little by little, fakir-like, I learned to control my heart rate, filling my medicine cabinet with little dropper bottles given to me by my homeopath neighbor. I wouldn't even go as far as the kitchen without my golden yarrow, star of Bethlehem, borage, or angelsword to hand. I also developed the strange habit of listening to romantic ballads. The effect of these on me was miraculous: I found them uplifting, to the point of actually being unsettling. Not only did they make me happy, they also made me feel good, good in a new, almost religious way. *God's help is nearer than the door,* an Irish proverb says. In short, I indulged in a little self-help.

I had gone full circle, an entire round-trip without barely leaving my room, and after a month of carefully combined yogic exercises, flower essences, and music, I was deposited back in my day-to-day as good as new, ready to insert myself in my routine again. Another disaster was the last thing I expected, but life, unyielding life, only went and doubled down on me. As my friend's grandmother says, "One piece of bad luck doesn't automatically mean there won't be more." The doorman at the newspaper offices, whose generally indifferent conduct was not so much automaton-like as like that of someone taking deadly nightshade on a regular basis, said I wasn't allowed in. When I asked why, the man took from his drawer a sheet of paper on which I saw words printed in elegant gothic lettering. He read them solemnly to me: "Last Tuesday, at three p.m., the management had to contract someone else at the last minute to cover the San Pablo Biennale." Enough said. I asked if I could at least go and collect my books. Really I wanted to do a little furtive observation, and I was sufficiently insistent that he eventually let me through. I should have remembered Enriqueta's advice when she said, never tackle an enemy at the end of a journey, unless it's your enemy who's the travel-weary one. I found a young man at my desk with cadaverous features and ambitious eyes. One look and I could tell he was a better example of the art-critic species than I could ever hope to be. I congratulated him, servilely, ironically. I shook his hand—his fingers as hard as needles on a spinning wheel. I felt my blood pressure drop. I bit my lip. Must be brave, I said to myself, and whatever you do don't let anyone see what you're really feeling. My books were in neatly stacked cardboard boxes outside the restrooms. The young guy offered to help me carry them out to the street, an obvious attempt to stop me from lingering; my now ex-colleagues watched me walk by with smiles on their faces, veritable theaters of lies. I was big enough by then to know that the truth is always something that does not smile. I finally made it out of that dump with my head held high.

On the street, I hailed a taxi whose tinted windows gave it an intriguingly covert air, and as I was inserting myself between my belongings on the back seat, I looked around to see the young critic slamming the door. I did not like his haste at all; the author of the drama in that scene should have been me, after all, it was my goodbye. Then an *organic* sensation came over me—to put it one way. Was I passing out again? Looking out the window, trying to understand, I then saw: it was my hand, the right one, and it had still been in the door as it shut; my fingers were being crushed between taxi door and frame.

But once more the medieval wheel of fortune spun—how many times had it done so those past months? How many more would it spin again that day? Boetius said: "You try to stop the wheel from spinning? Naïve mortal! If Fortune were to stop, it would be Fortune no longer." So I screamed, and the taxi driver, with his golden shoulder-length hair, flew to my aid like a very angel of Giotto, opening the guillotine door and, a second later, giving me a bag of ice cubes and ordering me to put my mangled hand inside. He got straight back in his seat and put his foot down so that the wheels screeched, as though we had suddenly joined a car chase. I gave him my address, but rather than go the direct route he went along parallel streets, seemingly in knowledge of a traffic jam somewhere. My vision went blurry as the city flew by outside, but I was calm; I felt I was being looked after for the first time in a very long time.

As the driver threaded his way between moving vehicles, he took me deep into the interior of his art. Perhaps this was in order to take my mind off the pain, perhaps to convert me to his faith—I've seen Brazilian ministers recruiting church members at hospitals: the unwell, those laid low by life, are easy targets. I say this because, in spite of his angelic aspect, the man was a ninjutsu expert and his tinted car an undercover weapon: his steering wheel concealed a katana sword under black velvet, there were nunchakus under the passenger seat, and the little Christmas baubles hanging from the rearview mirror hid various shining steel death stars. It was a subject I knew nothing about, but it would seem that ninjas first emerged in Japan during feudal times, when the peasantry rose up against an oppressive emperor. At first they used rakes, walking sticks, and scythes to fight with, but when their initial efforts were repelled they went away and became masters of espionage, disguise, and counterfeit. I became lost after that in certain historical details.

"Take my card," said the taxi-driver ninja when we got to my building. "I see you have enemies. Nobody's safe."

Later, on my balcony, feeding the pigeons the breadcrumbs of hot-dog buns, and both morally and physically paralyzed, I estimated that the young critic would be on the plane to the Brazil biennale at that moment. In all my years on the arts desk I had never managed a trip even as far as to Chivilcoy, but that was perhaps my own problem, not his, and as a tear slid down my cheek I asked myself if it might not be a crocodile's. One sometimes goes into character, and it can be difficult to tell the difference. So it was when I finally lost my job. My days as an art critic were over. A stroke of good luck? Or bad? Who, as the Chinese proverb says, can tell?

•

On the wall of my hotel room there is a mirror with beveled edges, and a number of traditional pampas prints depicting gauchos on horseback, bola lassos high in the air as they chase down ostriches, which dodge and feint their way across the land. There is also the Louis XVI desk, at which I never sit, and a blackout curtain I keep lowered. Halfway through the week, the concierge mentioned there was going to be a band playing. How interesting, I said, a band. Perhaps I'll come down for a listen. I said this with enthusiasm, almost as though I were a different person, as though trying different personalities on for size.

A few hours later, I put my fur coat on and, steeling myself, went down to the concert hall—which turned out to be a cold, badly lit room with lino flooring, a few small tables, and five or six gentlemen gathered around their blackish drinks. The waitress who brought my Bloody Mary agreed that it was a bad night for that time of year. The band turned out to be all women. Most of them wore blusher on their more-or-less wizened cheeks and most did not seem to take the performance tremendously seriously. I got back to my room with the strains of a possibly Hungarian ballad clanking around inside my brain.

And in that state I remained. During the night, unable to sleep, what could I not do? No evil act would have been beyond me, though at the same time—why not?—I felt equally capable of taking the Bible out of a drawer and dipping into the New Testament. There are moments when I think this hotel a kind of brushwood for larvae like me. The cleaners hardly ever come to my room and I have seen women with babies in their arms in the hallways but never heard any crying.

My insomniac nights are sometimes spent looking at my smile in the mirror. I try to correct it, to make it symmetrical, so that the two edges go up at the same time and to the same height as well; for my face to be harmonious. In any case, a smile is nothing but a mask. I know by now that the most sincere part of the face is the eyes. The bartender in the hotel lounge, a man by the name of Joe Navarro, told me that the eyes are the clearest barometer of our feelings. See something we like, and our pupils dilate; see something we don't, they contract. There's no way of controlling this. I suppose it is why those French seminarians from the nineteenth century, so partial to their divinely inspired intrigues, went around always with heads lowered.

But I don't wish to give the wrong idea. These conversations with the hotel employees are the exception to the rule. I have systematically avoided talking to anyone since I got here. I spend the majority of the time in bed—it's my own personal raft. I drift along on a sea of papers, a long way out from shore.

•

After the newspaper fired me, I was unemployed for a time. Not a good time. A moment came when I was little more than a corpse lying on the verge. Even the peaks of my former anxiety had gone, giving way to a general and constant low, an accumulated sensation of uselessness. It was a time when I felt the power of the mind and how it can, if one allows it, shake one anytime it wishes—I can think of no subtler way to put it. It was in an attempt to take the bull by the horns that I remembered a technique Enriqueta used when trying to focus. It consisted of hiding fifty grains of rice in different places around the house, in a shelf in the freezer, behind a vase, in a bathroom cupboard, under the pillow, inside a shoe; the possibilities were almost endless. She would hide them on a good day and then forget about them until the off-day came, the day when the equalizer went out, when she would recall her medication. The prescription was simple: she had to find each of the grains of rice one by one, all fifty, not stopping until all were found. "A search is a way of straightening you out," she said. "It keeps the thing at bay."

It might be that this memory precipitated all that followed, but there might also have been yet another, hidden deep in the layers of my unconscious. What's certain is that, late one day when I had the strong sense of needing to take decisive action on my own behalf, or there would soon be no way back, the thought came to me—not the most senseless of thoughts—of taking out the Rolodex I had hidden at the back of the wardrobe. I had removed it from Enriqueta's office after she died but never put it to use. I dragged a chair over and had to get up on tiptoes to pull it down. I nearly toppled off, but just caught myself. The Rolodex was heavier than I remembered, and its impractical design, both hard and soft at the same time, made it not very easy to carry. I put it down on my bed and looked at it with devotion, like a golden calf. I sat down next to it and spun the cards around, surveying the graveyard of names it contained. It came to a stop, like Pac-Man's wide-open mouth, on a yellow card.

I had to try several more of the cards. A lot of the numbers I called simply rang and rang, but some people picked up, though when they heard the name I put to them they just apologized and said they didn't know who I was talking about, while others still hung up before I'd got through my explanations. But every so often there would come the answer: "Ah, yes, of course . . . *her.*"

The Cloud of Unknowing

The advantage of interviewing older people is that you

can find out more about them than they can about you.

You can almost come up with a life story for yourself on

the spot, invent a whole eccentric past full of incredible

94

happenings. When I got to the bar, the waitress pointed me to a table next to the window where an overweight man, age uncertain, was hunched over a book. Germán had a white coat on and seemed to me straight out of one of Somerset Maugham's Malaya stories; he could just as easily have been sitting on the veranda of a bungalow sipping Singapore slings. He had been friends with the boyfriend. The boyfriend's friends always have something to say about the girl. I told him what it was I wanted to ask about. The name took him aback, even though I had mentioned it on the phone the night before. He repeated it to himself and, when the waitress came over, repeated it to her, too, like a password. She smiled at him. I could see that it was the two of them, and then me; I had to find a way to break the entente.

"What was she like? As good-looking as people say?"

"Oh, dazzling, and gloomy, and strange."

"She was your friend's woman."

"They weren't together by the time I met her, but she was still like a muse to him."

"In what way?"

"There was something of Lilith about her—the one whose fire illuminates but can also burn you. Sure, she had talent, but there are certain women destined to be remembered only for the affair they had with some celebrity or other . . ."

"I'm interested in her work."

"She wasn't."

"Really?"

"Really."

"Where was she from?"

"I don't know. She was a drifter. Anyway, in those days nobody asked that kind of thing."

"And why strange?"

"At first, the little things: she smoked Havanas, wore miniskirts. It's so difficult now, when people can have a chat about orgasms over a bowl of peanuts, to remember the force of those old taboos! People also said she was the first to bring marijuana into the country. Marijuana and condoms, which she and a friend sold at this chic clothes store over on Calle Montevideo. Then the really crazy stories started, her playing Russian roulette during drinking sessions, being into black magic."

"Who did she go around with?"

"She moved in various circles, but didn't belong to any of them. She was just as at home among the intellectuals who hung out at Bar Moderno as she was with the musicians down at La Perla. Then at the end of the sixties people got into shooting up, and she was all for that. Some paid a pretty heavy price for going down that road."

"And her?"

"I don't know, we didn't see her around in those days.

But something tells me she must have avoided the worst of it. She was a cerebral woman, she didn't let her passions rule her all the time. Do you know what I mean? She was in the self-preservation game, was only destructive up to a point. I think she went through a sort of golden era, and then a time of darkness, always existing slightly at the margins. Did you read Carlos Correa's book? He mentions her."

"Yes, I actually brought it with me . . . This is the part: '. . . the room the couple share will be stacked with antique, though not very fine furniture, supposedly from Japan, and, under the erotic bed, there will be a small crocodile—a real one—which makes a regular habit of jumping out at the three of us when we go to visit our friends. I now think the crocodile was more Renée's doing than Oscar's. He loved her a lot; we all did. And she lived with Oscar and, indifferent to what anyone else thought, pandered to that crocodile.'"

"There you have it; he knew her better than me. I was younger."

"But Correa isn't here . . . Is it true about the crocodile?"

"They said it was called Abdul—I never saw it—and that it would let you stroke it, but also that she kept a loaded gun on the table."

He fell silent and I, against all good judgment, asked, "Did you ever hear talk of her art forgery?"

"Of course."

"Ever see any of the pictures?"

"Never."

"But it was common knowledge?"

"We all knew. In those days, no one was going to be a Judas, the cops weren't our friends. It was seen as a good thing, the fact that she did these forgeries. See? I don't know if that was how she saw it at the time, or if it's the way it seems to me now. I sometimes wonder if art fraud wasn't the twentieth century's single greatest piece of art."

Again he fell silent, leaving me to wonder if this might not be some time-worn technique for getting the other person to speak. Eventually—not rushing—I filled the gap. But my anxiety won out.

"Do you think she's dead?"

"That I don't know. I liked her, I really did, but that isn't to say I knew her."

Another silence—I now saw these were spontaneous, not preplanned—there was nothing premeditated about the man. Not one for reflection.

"Look," he said, "I'm sorry, I thought I had more to tell you, but I now see that I don't. I was younger then and she had something of the aura of a legend. A legend from just five minutes before; that was what was strange about Renée."

•

Here was the inextricable mixture of poetry and truth of which all legends are made. One could do something with a story like this, I thought, getting up from the table—a thought that gradually took hold over the following days. I would go looking for Renée; I'd do whatever it took, go to the ends of the earth if necessary, and if she were still alive I would find her, would relieve her of her secrets, then turn them into a book. My ears had always pricked up when it came to the subject of genius and its nature.

A bar on Calle Arenales. I went inside and found several of the window tables occupied by women sitting on their own. A hunch told me which one she was, and I turned out to be right. Sylvia was tall and thin, with an aquiline nose and a shock of dark hair. She was dressed in black with dark glasses. The waiter came and put down two cups of coffee she had gone ahead and ordered.

"She was avant-garde, and completely unshakeable in that. They'll never catch me, she seemed to say. Anything commonplace, she was against it, against everything to do with promoting her own work, a stance she maintained with complete consistency." She glanced out the window before continuing: "I remember one time, we were at a party, Oscar had some other girl on his arm, and suddenly the whole place began to swell, it was like a rising wave, 'Here comes Renée, here comes Renée,' people said, and there she suddenly was, stepping through the door with that dark beauty of hers. She marched straight to the middle of the dance floor, straight up to Oscar, took him by the hand, and led him out. What do I know . . . There are certain passions that are beyond us to control, they simply arrive in the world, part of some bigger design."

I was making notes; often they're all that remains of a person.

"The love between them was always larger than life," she continued. "She had a temper. She said to me one day: 'I wonder sometimes where all this spite inside me came from.' It was like she had some incredible hardness within, a stoniness . . . I don't know."

"Did she show you her paintings?"

"When I met her, she was doing drawings in pencil, semi-surreal little things. But she had no interest in selling them."

"Showing them, or selling them?"

"Difficult to say. Who can be sure why anyone does anything? I just know she never showed me much of her work."

"And the paintings she forged?"

"Oh, that came afterward. Late sixties. At first it was a way to get by . . . Gómez Cornet, Gambartes, Spilimbergo. There was only one moral she lived by: get yourself out there, take what's yours. Not to say she wasn't principled about her forgeries, wasn't proud of them. I was sometimes the one who took them to sell at galleries."

"Did she make a living from it?"

"A sort of living, and more so over time—there was nothing systematic about it, in general she lived off thin air . . . Though people who live off thin air are often actually living off their family. I think her father had been in the army, because she was on some kind of military welfare. The last time she called me it was to do with the cats—one of her thousands of house cats had bitten her. I said, go and get yourself vaccinated, but she didn't want to. Frightened of doctors."

"And when was that call?"

"Must have been ten years ago . . . She'd just moved to the house that had belonged to her mother, near Chas Park. I remember she called me the night she moved in. She'd walked in to find some guy sitting in the living room, and he said to her, 'You can't be here anymore, go find yourself a bridge to live under.'"

"Was she unhinged? Did she see ghosts?"

"I don't think people who see ghosts are necessarily

unhinged. It can be good to see things; the visionary, the prophet, shamans, witch doctors, they all see things."

"Do you think she'll still be at that same address?"

"No . . . She could be anywhere."

"Do you have any photos?"

"Nothing." She shrugged. And after a pause: "Know what, though? If I did know where she was, I think I'd respect her wish to not be found. I'm going to go now, sorry, I've got things to do."

I watched from the table as she crossed the street. A car was coming, the light was green, but she crossed anyway, triumphantly—the car had to slam on its brakes. She was no longer young, but there was still the impunity of beautiful people in the way she walked.

Nicolás, eyes sparkling, watched the women coming into the bar. He was ninety years old and what little hair he had left was the color of a fly's wing. We were in Belgrano, not far from where the Hotel Melancholical had once stood.

"Ah, well, her skin was very dark brown, she had seductive lips, amazing legs . . . What a thing memory is, the way all the minor details simply vanish. Yes, she was intelligent, but not that coatrack kind of intelligence for just hanging ideas on; a crazier, more acute kind of intelligence. The first time I saw her was in El Moderno. She was at the bar. She had her hands in the pockets of her coat and a cigarette dangling from her lips. She knew full well the stir she was causing; she actually seemed a bit annoyed about it, though there was no way to play down her presence; all she had was her cigarette, and she could hardly have hidden behind that! I remember asking her what she'd been up to that day, and her saying she'd been at the fine arts college. That was a surprise, she could hardly have been more opposed to anything canonical, and a college? Far too formal for someone like her. When I said this, she just said, 'They teach me things, I like that.'"

"Was she as difficult as people say?"

"No, not at all. It was only her boyfriend she gave a hard time to. She found him weak, she ridiculed his need to please, looked down on him slightly for it. She didn't need to be liked by anyone: that was her strength."

"Did you ever see any of her pictures? Her, how can I put it, her *own* things?"

"Not many of them. In the place she lived on Calle Viamonte, she'd done this beautifully sweet face on one of the walls, but then when you went up close you saw it was bleeding from one of the eyes, blood pouring down onto the floor and running along like a river . . . I haven't thought about that in years."

"Did you see anything else in the place where she was living?"

"I don't remember now—amazing how it all fades! Wait, something I do remember is that she always had that book with her, *The Cloud of Unknowing*. Have you read it? One of the great mystical tomes."

"Never heard of it."

"*The Cloud* is no book for the uninitiated. Fortunately Renée was far from being that."

"In what sense?"

"At the time when I met her, she was doing strict exercises as a way of avoiding 'distractions.' That which the contemplatives described as being like a swarm of flies or froth floating on top of things; the unimportant stuff, in a word, nonsense to which our minds are slaves."

"Did she carry these mystical ideas over into her visual work?"

"I really don't know. She tended not to show me her paintings. She was really very shy."

"And why did she never exhibit?"

"I didn't ask. It was obvious she was more artistic than ambitious. Pride was something that blinded artists, she said. And that the best place to overcome pride was in a work of art. On top of that, between you and me, I think her work was too dark for widespread consumption."

•

A bookseller on Avenida Corrientes told me he had an aunt who'd been at the Pueyrredón school in the early seventies. She was very old now but still *compos mentis*.

Aunt Margarita's apartment was near Centenario Park. Rainy Sundays in that part of the city are the muted gray of towns in central Europe. On my way there I walked past the naval hospital, one of Clorindo Testa's creations. I always found the portholes on the frontage striking, the boat resemblance. What person would want to be ill at sea? An overemphasis on the aesthetic has the propensity to come through as a demented love of form.

The clouds were high in the sky, wet shadows lay across the street. A woman came forward between frosted panes of glass. When she opened the door I found before me a slight, elderly woman with green eyes, face covered in a multitude of wrinkles, and, hanging over the left shoulder of her blue dress, a ginger plait that gave her the look of a farmer's wife. She asked me to come up.

An easel with a painting mounted on it stood on the gloomy landing. Everything inside was covered in a fine layer of dust. There were two armchairs with threadbare crochet covers, and ornamental plates on the walls with hand-painted sayings: "Every rose has its thorns," "Lay the axe to the root," "God tempers the wind to the shorn lamb."

We sat down at a table and I could feel the cobwebs
dangling down over my head. The aunt brought a wicker
tray with teacups, tea bags, and a little basket with slices
of toast. But there was neither butter nor jam or anything
else to spread on the toast, and we were to wait for someone called Mónica to bring hot water in a thermos; the
building had been without gas for weeks. In one corner,
on another easel, another painting, an abstract by the same
hand as the one on the landing.

"Renée? Do you remember her?"

"Of course. She was older than me."

"Ah, I thought you'd be the same age."

"No, no, I was younger."

"But were you friends at the school?"

"I don't remember her going to the school. She spent
her time on Avenida Corrientes, displaying her wares."

"Displaying her wares?"

"You know . . . streetwalking. She sold her body." She
gave a gentle smile to cushion this.

"Ah."

"Why are you interested in that woman?"

I explained it again, to the best of my abilities. She
listened impassively before responding.

"That boyfriend of hers, Oscar, he had a lot of different girls . . . In fact, I was one of them."

This I hadn't expected.

"In his eyes, the fact that I wouldn't sleep with him without getting married made me bourgeois. 'Let's get married, then,' he said. It's awful—I lost all his letters."

"People say Renée was a virtuoso painter."

"People? Who?" Aunt Margarita scrunched up her nose as though she could smell an onion. "There were a lot of virtuoso painters in those days."

"But not so many women . . . Not really outstanding ones, at least."

"Outstanding! That's going a bit far! She was good-looking, but in a provincial way—those big cheekbones. There was a write-up on her in a magazine once and the journalist described her as having the nose of a small puma. I cut that out, but threw it away when I married someone else."

"A small puma's nose—sounds nice to me."

"Think so?"

Gone was the sweet old Aunt Margarita of a moment before. An edge had entered her voice.

"Did you know she did Berni's paintings for him? And he'd just sign them, and sell them like they were his own work?"

I held her gaze.

"I just feel," she said, "that if a person paints more copies than paintings of their own, a moment arrives when that person turns hollow."

"Perhaps—not necessarily, though."

"Want to know what people said at the time? That she could only do forgeries because when she produced paintings of her own, they always came out dead. Tell me, have you found out if she's still alive?"

"Alive and kicking," I lied.

"Alzheimer's got her?"

"Far from it."

"If she's alive, what do you need me for?"

"Oh, you know, there are still a few gaps in the picture."

The doorbell rang. Mónica turned out to be a long-standing student. She had a thermos of hot water and a poppyseed cake. But my appetite was gone. They started talking about the proliferation of Chinese supermarkets. I pretended to be interested while looking at the paintings on the walls, which were all atrocious. Not that I said so. After a short while I made my excuses and got up to leave.

Since there was no doorman on Sundays, Aunt Margarita had to see me out. The flesh-and-blood Aunt Margarita, together with the one in the black-stained mirror of the elevator, looked at me like a pair of chaste nuns: indifferent to physical contact, not susceptible to human warmth. The elevator gave a jolt and, as suddenly as hail, stopped.

"Find something else to write about," the real Aunt

Margarita and her double both whispered. "That woman is no character for a book."

There's nothing like being told not to open a door to intensify your desire to open it. It's the same the world over. By now it seemed to me that the abiding impression she had left was not inaccurate; Renée must have been a woman, or something far better, or something far worse.

Luisa had been her dance partner. She and Renée had taken modern-dance classes in a dingy studio beneath the Lavalle cine club. She had been elegant once; she showed me a photo to prove it. If the person in the picture was the same as the one before me, the transformation was astonishing: the supple sylph had now become a portly general issuing orders, even down to the right way to ask questions. (In this she slightly resembled Maria de' Medici in Rubens's portrait of her in old age.)

She said to me, "No, no, *no*. You've got it all wrong. She was a good person who sometimes painted evil things. When she and Oscar fought, she'd go off with an Italian called Livio. And Livio wasn't into women, but made an exception with her. He took her to his house in Montes de Oca, which was the home of his adoptive father,

Wilcock, who was in Italy. I went to Montes de Oca a couple of times. They were looked after by an old French maid who wore a white linen cap. Jeanette, she was called, and she spent the whole time keeping the fire going—the fire smoked, it was like she was curing herself to be eaten. There was a small porcelain plate on the landing on which Jeanette left ten centavos for the pharmacist who came to do her daily insulin injection. Livio went for supper at Bioy Casares's house one night. Borges, as ever, was also dining there. After dessert, Livio read a Wilcock poem, one in Italian called 'Al fuoco.' I was at Montes de Oca when Wilcock got back and told the tale: 'Borges *ha detto*, how curious that when a poem appeals to us very much, we think to go and make another exactly the same.' 'Ah!' said Renée. 'I know exactly what he means!' And that's what happened, precisely as I'm telling you: I was there, and it features in Bioy's diaries as well."

"Did she ever talk to you about *The Cloud of Unknowing*?"

"I've no idea what that is."

"She never mentioned an interest in mysticism?"

"Never, but you've seen how people are: nothing if not diverse. We used to cycle out to El Ancla, a beach in Vicente López, and we'd be sunbathing and meanwhile the two of them would squabble over who was the lovelier. They shared a hedonistic kind of love that wasn't passion but something calmer. In their official loves, it was different. 'Progress in love'—according to Wilcock—'consists of successfully finding people who are like gunshots, like cannon blasts, like nitroglycerine cartridges, like torpedoes, like atomic bombs, and, finally, like hydrogen bombs.' Oscar showed up at Montes de Oca one day, and it was fireworks. Jeanette's little porcelain plate didn't survive. Renée fled in shame.

"Where did she learn to forge paintings? Well, any art school is a school for potential forgers. They all encourage copying because there's no other way to teach art but by imitating the past. She was one of Polesello's cohort—she was a classmate of his—but she wasn't like him. He'd finish a painting and put a price on it. Not her. I don't think she was able to let go of her creations. She tried other things besides painting. There was the Vignes gallery, for example, a little place tucked away on Calle Corrientes y Maipú. The owner was a guy called Llinás, and he had a project going in those days called 'The Plastic Arts in Plastic.' Remember those acrylic key rings you used to get with butterflies inside them? Well, Renée came up with the idea of putting a man inside a plastic cube. She made the relevant inquiries. Seems you had to put in an extraction pump to drain the liquids created by the body decomposing. But the hardest part was getting hold of a body: it had to be a thirty-year-old man,

tall, good-looking, and dead of natural causes—no signs
of violence. Llinás said he'd heard of somebody in Paris
exhibiting the exact same thing, and canceled the show.

"Then, later on, she painted some gargantuan paintings but didn't show them. What she did make money
from were the forgeries. She sold them with papers cooked
up for her by the critic García Martínez. He was divine,
that man! Died in La Paz."

"In Bolivia?"

"No, no, no. In La Paz the *bar*. In the restroom."

These people conducted their lives in bars. That was
where they talked to one another, smoked one another's
cigarettes, drank hard—so much so that they seemed to
live in a cloud, like the Greek gods in one of Tiepolo's
paintings deliberating over the lives of mortals. All that
smoke—it was also like a curtain shielding them from the
world. These were bars in which you could barely move
for people, boys and girls in their twenties who thought
themselves brilliant, though not all of them were. Most
had literary interests but earned a living in advertising.
There could be a ghost tour of the bars that have disappeared. None of them are what they once were, most have
been modernized, depersonalized, all with the same white
operating-theater lights, all with the same artificial plants.

But there was a time when the bar was one's home away from home; the home people actually wanted to live in. Those at the Di Tella Institute congregated at Bar Moderno at 900 Calle Maipú, which is almost on Calle Paraguay; the rebel poets at La Paz on Corrientes and Montevideo; the students from the philosophy and literature faculty at Coto Grande at 500 Paraguay; the musicians at La Perla— they'd head there at 4 a.m. when La Cueva shut. It wasn't all completely cut and dried, of course, they intersected, they defected, they cross-pollinated. The bohemian life was one of agitation, violence, full of extremes. Everything was writ large: arguments were heated, victories brutal, betrayals truly epic. But I can't be exact about these things, I'm not going to lie. I wasn't there, this is only a reconstruction effort, a last-ditch attempt to bring back the ambience of those days.

Edgardo was at La Biela; I recognized him by the white trousers he'd often worn at openings. One moment his gaze was calm, a second later it turned troubled, as though the mere mention of Renée acted on him like an effervescent pill dropped in a glass of water. Things long since deposited as sediment were brought straight back to the surface.

"I remember, I remember perfectly," he said. "She had

this special *density* to her. She lived in an apartment on Calle Viamonte. It was down some steps, and all shadowy inside . . . but the darkness wasn't negative, quite the opposite. Here, I've brought the poster from her first exhibition—I designed it."

I took the rolled-up sheet and opened it out. The poster was in good condition. There was a picture of a bird in suit and tie, set inside an oval. Around it were the words "Drawings. Lirolay Gallery, Buenos Aires. May 26–June 8, 1965."

"Ah," I said. "So she did show her work at some point."

"Of course. What did you think? We all wanted to exhibit. This was an individual show. Probably her first, I don't know if it was her last."

"And what kind of work was she showing?"

"Pictures of bird-men. Their beaks were like those of crows, or hawks, maybe—I don't know much about birds."

"Do you remember if anything sold?"

"No idea. Nobody kept track of that, it wasn't really the point."

"Do you remember seeing other drawings?"

"Yes, she often showed me her work, although I never got a very clear view of it. Like I say, the house was always dark . . . So you saw everything, but at the same time you only got a glimpse."

"Would you say she had talent?"

"She had talent that wasn't of this time."

"Did you see her again?"

"Never."

"I am a camera," Roberto could have said of himself, but instead he said to me, over the phone.

"She was at the intersection of many moments in history. I remember we were having dinner in a little place on Avenida Corrientes and Renée came in, sat down across from Oscar, and started blowing smoke in his face. Oscar suddenly jumped up, flipped the table over, all the plates went flying. 'A Greco, a Greco,' everyone started shouting."

"A performance, like one of Alberto Greco's . . ."

"Yes, it was a very performative time. I can see her now, coming out of the Teatro Colón, a group of girls flitting around her. A dark fairy with her entourage of nymphs . . . She saw me and waved, and I felt like I was in a scene from a Dario Argento film. She was possessed, that woman."

"Possessed?"

"Oh yes, definitely something witchy about her."

"Do you know if she's still alive?"

"No idea. She always was quite the recluse. Ah . . ."

"Yes?"

"I remember she also made some bead necklaces, all

lovely bright colors, but I don't know if that's any help with your portrait . . ."

Roberto gave the impression that he knew more than he was ever going to divulge.

In my adolescence there was a game people played in bars. A paper napkin would be laid taut over the top of a glass and secured with a rubber band, and a ten-centavo piece would be placed in the middle. People took it in turns to touch the end of their lit cigarettes to the napkin around the outside of the coin, without—and herein the virtually erotic suspense generated by the game—letting the coin drop. If too large a hole was burned, the coin would fall, and that player lost. My search for Renée reminded me of that game, with every new fact, every anecdote or snippet of information like another hole in the napkin; bringing me closer to her, but precariously so. I wanted to get closer and at the same time I did not.

"Where are you?" I asked the air. "Where have you hidden yourself away?" People create ties, nobody lives a life in complete isolation. But Renée would appear to have been the exception. Her only friendships were fleeting, people were soon dispatched. Such people do exist, going through life alone. "For to be social is to be forgiving," says Robert Frost in "The Star-Splitter." Did she not trust anyone? Did people grow tired of her? Did she grow tired of others? Renée put so much distance between herself and everyone else that it was impossible to break through. But even such people leave some kind of trace.

I had been progressing through my list of possible interviewees with surprising speed. Every bit the novice, I wasn't recording any audio, and the notes I took were almost illegible. People's voices became muddled in my memory and I couldn't tell who had said what. My inquiries were becoming a black box: a device that registers many conversations but that rarely produces anything of any use.

"I'm sorry that I can't help. Years ago someone told me about her, but I can't now remember who. I imagine that if she's still alive, she must be very old. In an institution, an old people's home, or six feet under—I wouldn't know."

"An old people's home. Almost certainly."

"She's a Scorpio, one of the most seductive creatures on earth but at the same time one of the most poisonous."

"Did you look at the Tanguito book? Pintos' is good,

a group biography that re-creates those times—a time of peace and love but also of rupture. This, for example, is Sweet Jorgito: 'We were going over to this nurse's place— he was also blind and a pianist—to shoot up. The first time, I went outside and saw Jimi Hendrix with the tree on the corner for his amplifier. When the heroin came on the scene, big gatherings started happening less. It was more a thing of getting together at people's houses. There were only ten of us at the start. Ten, maximum. I think the first to start were Tango, Silvia Washington, Renée, and me.'

"With her it was like, *something wicked this way comes* . . . There was a guy who was dying to get with her, and when he finally got her back to his apartment one night, she, as foreplay, cut him with a knife on the back . . . Like Gombrowicz said, dream or reality? Hard to tell with her. Urban myths, probably . . . like the army keeping an alien's body in a deep freeze in Patagonia. That kind of deal.

"A group of us went to Lobos once with the idea of setting up a hippie commune. There were something like two thousand people around the lake. You could see lights inside people's tents and in the middle of the night helicopters came and started circling overhead. The whole thing was Renée's doing, and while we stood around the bonfire, a rumor started up: 'Renée's in that

tent, no, she's in that one, no, that one.' No one eve
tually saw her."

I went on, no longer wanting to, and not expecting anything to come of it either, which I called being disciplined.
I gathered these disjointed images, supplying them with a
sort of coherence comprehensible only to me—or so it
began to feel, though also in no clear way. Some people
see memory as a telescope capable of capturing the past as
precisely as the Hubble telescope's photograph does the
Pillars of Creation, and say that a sustained effort of concentration and will is all that's needed. Memory must have
a good PR agent, because in reality, as an instrument of
optical precision, it seems to me little better than a fairground kaleidoscope. To reconstruct an experience on the
basis of images stored in our brains at times borders on
hallucination. We do not recover the past, we *re-create* it:
an act of dramaturgy if ever there was one. Memory edits
things, colors them, mixes cement with the rainbow, does
whatever's needed to make the story work.

The paranoia set in—as it does anytime one finds oneself lying in wait; a point comes when one learns to live
with it, even forming a fondness for it. ("Paranoia is the
muse of inspiration," said Tanguito.) The paranoiac thinks
she feels some latent sense of something, the reason for

the world's form, a pattern, some implacable logic, and the ambient scenes, people, and events begin to link together, creating a final image, a sun from which all rays issue and to which they all return. When in reality there is no such thing out there: life is definitively without shape, one stupid event after another, with barely any relation between the different parts. The paranoiac is the ultimate romantic.

I was reading a lot in those days, though rarely did I finish a book. This usually consisted of opening one at random, allowing its substance to suffuse me for a number of hours, and then simply putting it aside the very next day. It soon became clear that while I was reading, my brain was still involved in the search. I read an old book on falcons: "Observe that when a species is approaching extinction this means not only a numerical decline but a semantic one as well. The rarer an animal becomes, the fewer meanings are associated with it. In the end its rarity is the only thing that defines it." I read a poem by Cherubina de Gabriak: "In the sky there is a fluttering layer—a face—I did not see." I read T. H. White's *The Book of Merlyn*: "To disbelieve in original sin, does not mean that you must believe in original virtue. It only means that you must not believe that people are utterly wicked." I read *Less Than One* by Joseph Brodsky: "No life is destined to be preserved, and unless one is a pharaoh there is no reason to aspire to becoming a mummy." I read in the *Argentinean Navy Glossary of Nautical Terminology*: "'Underwater ship' is the name for the part of the boat beneath the waterline, the part hidden from view that is fundamental to the stability of the vessel." Did they not all have some bearing, whether tangential, oblique, or entirely direct, on the search I was involved in?

Such was my state when I came across a biography of William Blake. The story of this book has hardly any bearing on my main argument, while nonetheless being so instructive that I make no apology for summarizing it here.

One clear-skied morning in 1860 Dante Gabriel Rossetti received a letter from Alexander Gilchrist, a young art critic who had gained notoriety a few years earlier following his study of William Etty, a painter who had scandalized the Royal Academy with explicit nudes on enormous canvases. Gilchrist now had a new obsession. He wanted to write the biography of William Blake, the English artist also known as Mad Blake who had been a kind of spiritual guide for the Pre-Raphaelites. Gilchrist had found *The Book of Job* in a London bookshop and been unable to get the images of that "chronicle of an enlightenment" out of his head. To enter the mind of the artist, Gilchrist needed to study the notebook that had belonged to the painter and was now in Rossetti's possession, and jealously guarded by him.

The moment Gilchrist walked in, Rossetti knew he was in the presence of a kindred spirit. Rossetti found his long neck, Adam's apple, and sad eyes reassuring, and a week later he had given him carte blanche to go through all the papers. Gilchrist imbibed the manuscript, or it imbibed him. When he surfaced again, his obsession with Blake was sealed. He married Anne Burrows soon afterward, and his idea of a honeymoon was to go to London to look at engravings and carry out interviews. By the time his research was complete, he had a contract with the publishing house Macmillan.

Two years later, and with the book half-complete, Gilchrist was exhausted. He was penniless, and already a father of four. He lay in bed with fever for days at a time. Then his wife took the reins. She copied out manuscripts, looked up dates, worked on preparing the index. The publishing house, alarmed at Gilchrist's stop-start progress, began to apply pressure, and Gilchrist promised it would have the book within a year. He should have known that the worst plan is having any plan at all: his eldest daughter soon came down with scarlet fever, and Gilchrist himself fell ill once more. Ten days later he entered a coma. Anne wrote, "His mind is utterly worn down with the work, the fever burns him like a flame. Four days of delirium, then apoplexy, then the end: unspeaking, but with a look of loving recognition, he passed away. It was savage stormy, November 30, 1861, the night his spirit went up."

Gilchrist was thirty-three when he died. Blake's great biographer left his book unfinished but his widow decided to go on with it; she was well familiar with his way of working. Now she had to see if she could imitate his voice. The second volume was ready a year later. The *Life* was published in 1863, and it was the first attempt to set down Blake's career, he whom Chesterton called "a red-hot cannon ball," who expressed himself in apocalyptic images, who believed that death was no more than passing from one room to another, and who claimed to have his poems dictated to him by his dead brother. Unlike many Victorian biographies, it had a lively prose style, and succeeded in showing that there was nothing in Blake that lacked structure or focus, nothing that did not cohere, and what is more, that he had a scheme for explaining the universe in its entirety. It was only that no one could understand it.

Life of William Blake, "Pictor Ignotus," one of the most extreme cases of an artist being rescued from oblivion, was written in conditions of penury. "None but I could have done it," Anne said to her editor on delivering the manuscript. "Gilchrist's spirit was with me all the time I wrote. When I stopped, I felt him going away." It was a collaboration between a dead husband and his widow. Such things were still believed in. Then, "The heavens proclaimed," says Hazlitt, and that was the moment at which people stopped believing in the supernatural.

This Señor Ramos

There was something pathetic about my quest, I can see

it now. Perhaps it was *Sehnsucht* that pushed me on—the

German term denoting a melancholic desire for some in-

tangible thing. C. S. Lewis described it as the inconsolable longing for something though we don't even know what it is. At root, for me, Renée was a mental state, a cloud on the horizon.

Of course, I wasn't completely unaware of this possibility, and although I began to suspect that my attempted biography was coming apart in my hands, still I wasn't prepared to let it go. It served to thread my days together, it gave me a purpose, a reason for being—all that I had recently lost. The search itself provided me with a direction, and I kept finding new things, however trivial, because Renée's reputation was such that people would associate her with any strange anecdote from the time. You only really needed a couple of them to summarize that woman's life. But who in reality was Renée? That, nobody seemed to know.

1. She was solitary but never alone.
2. She had a destructive side, like the vast majority of people with talent.
3. She stole a copy of *The Human Mind* by Dr. Karl Menninger from a friend's library. In the prologue to this description of deviant behavior, it says, "The idea of the normal repels me. Anyone who achieves anything in this life is, a priori, abnormal."
4. In the seventies, she informed on a lot of people

in exchange for drugs. A persistent claim. These are accusations, no proof exists.

5. She slept in the daytime because, as Wilcock says, "Nobody has ever seen black flowers, at least not in daylight."

6. She needed a filling at one point, but the dentist couldn't come in time. Renée fashioned a make-shift filling out of wax herself. It was only 6°C that night, but in the bar she ordered whiskey on the rocks: hot coffee was liable to melt the ersatz filling.

7. Meanings shift around when it comes to Renée: bad can be good, good can be bad. Like in prison slang.

8. She sometimes mentioned her father, who had been a naval officer, and her mother, who was very beautiful. But none of this was ever confirmed.

9. She lived at the Hotel Melancholical in the early sixties. The Mariette Lydis that presided over the dining room was her first ever forgery.

The night has a strange effect on the mind. One night a couple of months into my search, I had a dream. Two women were standing talking on a wooden bridge, lean-ing on the rickety rail. A lake stretched out before them. One was older than the other, quite a lot older, which

was clear from the whiteness of her hair and her lack of a
clearly defined waist, which in profile gave her the look of
a chess piece—a rook. From a distance, from their complete stillness, one might have mistaken them for lovers. I
didn't have a clear view but knew who they were. A brisk
wind began to blow, the trees protested, shaking their
branches, and as the temperature dropped Mariette Lydis
took out her old immigrant fur coat and gave it to Renée:
she showed her the European method of putting a coat
on while keeping hold of the ends of your shirtsleeves.
Dreams being what they are, suddenly it was Enriqueta
and me on the bridge struggling to put the coat on as
clouds raced overhead, assuming new shapes with every
instant. A whole pantomime of fairly ridiculous shoving
and pulling began between us and in the end we fell in the
lake, at which point I woke up.

I got out of bed feeling troubled, my spirit unquiet.
The Egyptian pharaoh was also shaken by his dreams,
but he had Joseph there to interpret them for him, and I
didn't even have a psychoanalyst on hand to rebuff mine as
"overly obvious." I made do with my books. They say that
detectives go on investigating even in their sleep, following
clues in unconscious material that doesn't surface by day.

These two women could not have been more different.
Mariette Lydis and Renée. Thirty years separating them;
one European, one South American; one an icy blonde,

the other with her torrent of dark hair; one the eternal little-girl dreamer, the other a realist femme fatale. And yet this curious similarity in the structures of their minds.

As when Andrei Bely and Aleksandr Blok sealed their friendship by swapping shirts, the exchange of clothes stood for them stepping into each other's skin. There was some intimate connection between them; it was no stranger that Renée was working with when she produced her counterfeit Lydises. I mulled over a number of ideas, keeping in mind one of Marcus Aurelius's first principles: simplicity. Where could they have met? At an opening at the Di Tella Institute? They were both around in the vibrant early 1960s, they shared that much, but they belonged to different tribes, one rubbing shoulders with the chic intelligentsia, the other with the roughest and readiest of bohemians; I discounted the idea. At Lydis's classes? That seemed more promising . . . Would Renée have been a life model? A student? A lover? Could Lydis have been the secret leader of the Melancholical Forgers, as suggested by Enriqueta at one point? How strange the way one forgets the things one knows, and appropriates things one has read before, forgetting completely where they came from. Or indeed, a third option, could they have met at the collector's estate? Did all the paintings of the time not pass through there? Perhaps the estate owner, himself drawn into some infamous art fraud litigation a while later, had introduced the two of them, imagining the connection being mutually beneficial to them in the future. I had no proof, but according to Calasso, that which the mind sees when it makes a connection, it never forgets.

It was this last intuition that led me to the National Criminal Appeals Chamber. I went looking for proceedings files, wanting to see if I would find anything to link the collector and these two women. "Many unthought-of connections come to light when that rock is overturned," Enriqueta had once said to me.

So it was that I stumbled upon six separately tied sheafs of papers, a thousand or so yellowing pages in all, which crumbled at the slightest touch like the layers of an onion. Here follows, for anyone with the patience to read it all, a selection of quotes summarizing the judgment on Federico Manuel Vogelius in the case of the counterfeit Figaris. It is not the whole story, but which one ever is?

NATIONAL CRIMINAL COURT OF
PRELIMINARY INVESTIGATIONS
Plaintiff: Damián Bendahan
Accused: Federico Manuel Vogelius
Case type: Fraud
Date: December 23, 1966
Crime: Sale of fake paintings
Judge: Héctor Dionisio Rojas Pellerano

Damián Bendahan: Witness Statement

ID: 1,262,134

In the city of Buenos Aires, Federal Capital of the Argentine Nation, this 23rd day of December 1966, it being 11 o'clock in the morning, the court heard the testimony of an individual, who first swearing to tell the truth regarding what he may know or be asked about, stated his name as Damián Bendahan, being of Argentine nationality, fifty-two years of age, civil status married, and by profession a civil engineer. He stated that he was for many years an associate of Señor Federico Manuel Vogelius in various companies. That because of this he was aware that Señor Vogelius collected the work of various artists, Pedro Figari in particular. That in 1960 he began acquiring from Señor Vogelius some paintings by Figari, finally amounting to eleven. Given the friendly relations between the two, he never asked for receipts. Later on, finding himself in financial difficulty, Bendahan asked Señor Fidel Rodríguez, who had formerly been in the employ of Señor Vogelius, to take the paintings to Municipal Bank to deposit as securities for a cash loan. A number of days later this bank communicated to him that other, identical paintings were already being held there, having been deposited in the past by Señor Vogelius, also as securities for a loan. All the paintings deposited by Bendahan were shown to be forgeries. That this is all he has to say on the matter.

131

Police Corporal Mancini: Statement

This 26th day of December 1966. Stated name as Alfredo Pedro Mancini, of Argentine nationality, thirty-seven years of age, civil status married, and by profession a police corporal. Stated that he made himself present at the property at 1330 Calle Cerrito. In said place, without revealing his identity as a police officer, was attended by a woman who made it known to him that Señor Vogelius had early that morning left for Punta del Este, Uruguay.

Present

This 27th day of December 1966. The examining magistrate states that the individual by the name Federico Manuel Vogelius has presented himself to the court of his own free will. As a precaution he is being detained and is at the disposal of the court. At 19:30 hours, the examining magistrate addressed the detained individual.

Federico Manuel Vogelius: Witness Statement

Argentine, married, forty-eight years of age, surveyor and accountant by profession, who with respect to the charges under investigation and for the purpose of clarifying his part, makes the following known: that he has in the past been the proprietor of a factory dedicated to the making of plastic sheeting, and the same of a cereal company, of various lumber mills, a dried-vegetables company and a doll-making factory. That in 1946 he went into business with the engineer Bendahan in an aluminum-sheeting venture, the company they created being called Alsico. That since 1952 he has dedicated himself to the collecting of first editions of books and of paintings, his principal interest being in the painter Pedro Figari.

Expert Witness

Dr. Marcelo Terán, the clerk, went to Municipal Bank, accompanied by the experts designated to examine the paintings belonging to Señor Bendahan, following which an exchange of opinions took place and this was recorded by stenography:

SEÑOR PAYRÓ: In my view these pictures are not at all good.

SEÑOR STEIN: This is a complicated matter, we can't jump to conclusions. I must consult my manual; there would need to be suitable evidence. I do not understand precisely what it is that the court wants to know.

SEÑOR PAYRÓ: To determine whether they are originals or not.

SEÑOR STEIN: I believe it could be argued that among the eleven works there is one that is both authentic and not at all good.

SEÑOR FEINSILBER: The court has no interest in whether the painting is good or not.

SEÑOR STEIN: And what if the painting is partially incomplete?

DR. TERÁN: Do not concern yourself with that; our remit is legal conclusions alone.

SEÑOR STEIN: You are not at all interested in the quality of the painting, how baffling.

The experts concluded: *These paintings are crude imitations of masterpieces. Executed by imitating aspects of authentic paintings, lacking in pictorial elegance, tonally clashing, mawkish in execution, and clumsy in the application of the paint.*

Señor Vogelius: Witness Statement, further
That among the places he went to acquire paintings was the establishment of Señor Ramos, Uruguayan, approximately thirty-five years of age, dark-skinned, 1.65 m in height, mustache, oiled black hair, "provincial-looking." Señor Vogelius states that he bought from this Señor Ramos cigarettes and imported whiskey and, on several occasions, paintings by Figari. That one day, in the middle of 1956, Señor Ramos made him a proposition, offering him some twenty Figari paintings at a total cost of 120,000 pesos. The witness not being in a position financially to assume this cost alone, he suggested to Señor Bendahan that they go in together. They divided the pictures, with eleven going to Señor Bendahan, no more than seven to Señor Vogelius.

Early in 1962, a lot came up at an auction of Figari's work, which included several paintings identical to the ones he had acquired from Señor Ramos. Upon seeing these, the witness determined that the paintings in his possession were copies. This he communicated to Señor Bendahan, who asked if he was still in contact with Señor Ramos. The witness said that he was. The three agreed to meet at the offices on Calle Maipú. At this meeting, Señor Bendahan and Señor Vogelius demanded their money back from Señor Ramos, to which he acceded, returning almost the entire sum. After this, Señor Vogelius destroyed the copies in his possession, and suggested Señor Bendahan do the same. Señor Vogelius also asked that he keep the affair a secret, given the damage it could do to his reputation as a collector.

Señor Bendahan: Witness Statement

That as regards this Señor Ramos of whom Señor Vogelius speaks, he does not know who he is, nor has he ever seen him. And that it would be ridiculous to think that a person of Señor Vogelius's prowess in matters of art could acquire paintings from a stranger who is also a purveyor of contraband cigarettes and whiskey.

Saúl Posternak (accountant, employee at Alisco): Statement

The witness recalls that a person would periodically appear at the offices with cigarettes and alcohol for sale. He believes he would be able to recognize this Señor Ramos were he to see him again. States that he was neither well-dressed nor scruffy, not a person of any standing, neither good-looking nor ugly, but simply average, regular-looking. He cannot remember whether he had a mustache but he believes not. That he once saw him enter the building with Figari paintings and put them on the table in the boardroom.

Artist's sketch

To better place this Señor Ramos, the court, with the assistance of the police forensics division, calls the accused. This is the impression obtained by Deputy Inspector Juan Edgardo Fourcade, prepared using details supplied by Señor Vogelius.

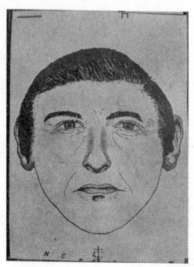

Señor Bendahan: Witness Statement

That it is his understanding that there have been other
victims of Señor Vogelius, in particular with respect to
an exhibition of Figari's work at the National Museum of
Modern Art in Paris.

Miguel Lermon: Witness Statement

That in May 1960 a Pedro Figari retrospective was held at
the National Museum of Modern Art in Paris. The person organizing the exhibition was the businessman Señor
Vogelius, who early in 1960 called him on the telephone
to ask to be lent three Figaris for display at the exhibition.
Señor Vogelius explained that he himself would take them
by airplane, and for this reason they must be removed from
their frames. At the conclusion of the exhibition, Vogelius called him on the telephone to say the return of the
paintings would be somewhat later than anticipated due to
some difficulties locating the corresponding frames. Also,
that the Paris show had been a great success. Within a
month Señor Vogelius again called him to say he would
be coming by to return the paintings. Later that day Señor
Vogelius arrived at the home of the witness but remained
in the entrance hall, where the lighting was poor, and—
while at no point asking to see the witness's receipts of
sale—offered to buy the paintings from him. The witness
said he did not wish to sell. The witness said that when he

came to look at his pictures in the daylight, he detected that something was awry. "It was like somebody having switched your child for another in the night," he said. He compared the paintings against photographs he happened to have had taken before their departure to Paris, and could see that the ones now in his possession were forgeries. He decided not to say anything to Vogelius, because his lawyer advised him that the evidence was insufficient, but among art buyers word began to circulate that all the paintings provided in good faith for the Paris exhibition had there been copied, and these copies then returned to the owners in place of the originals. Figari always painted on thick cardboard, and this could have been sliced down the middle, leaving thereby two halves: the idea being that Vogelius had kept the originals minus the backing (the forging of rear labels is a most straightforward activity) and returned the other (forged) half, newly affixed to the original backing.

Señor Vogelius: Witness Statement

On being returned from Paris, the paintings were taken to the Witcomb Gallery, where Señor Juan Fernández was tasked with restoring them to their original frames. This being done, the paintings were returned to their respective exhibitors and owners. The thought never occurred to the witness that the paintings had been forged. Had there been any fraudulent dealings, the Witcomb would be the place to inquire about them. Señor Fernández would need to be questioned. Señor Fernández, however, is dead.

Authorization
Señor Vogelius requests authorization to travel to Mexico on business for a period of twenty days.

Permission
Permission for the defendant to travel to Mexico is denied. He is to be notified.

Copy of Figari exhibition catalogue (National Museum of Modern Art) attached
with, on the cover, in Señor Vogelius's handwriting and among several other notes, the words "Jorge Demarchi, 2244 Juncal." Police inquiries suggest that this name and address belong in reality to Jorge Sangorrín, which individual is allegedly involved in international fraud, and currently fugitive, and was an associate of Señor Vogelius at the Chaumier nightclub on Calle Tres Sargentos.

Dr. Francisco de la Vega, Lawyer: Restitution
Upon seizure of property from my client's address on Calle Pueyrredón, an authentic work by the painter Marc Chagall, which is not connected with the present case,

was taken in error. I hereby request the return, with no further delay, of said work and that it is borne in mind the damage and harm done to my client by the involvement, in proceedings of this nature, of a work so valuable in the international market.

Juan Pedro Kramer: Witness Statement

That paintings belonging to him were requested to be shown at the Paris exhibition but that he did not agree to lending them. That one year later, in 1961, the National Museum of Fine Arts in Buenos Aires requested to borrow the works for an exhibition, to which he acceded, but that, soon after the exhibition opened, he went to the museum and on seeing that a large number of the Figaris on show were not authentic, among them many of those that had been in the Paris exhibition, he resolved not to lend his own works.

Accusation

The owners of the jewelry store at 933 Calle Patricios made themselves present at Precinct 25, where they accused Rodolfo A. Ruiz Pizarro of selling three counterfeited paintings by Pedro Figari. Señor Ruiz Pizarro was prosecuted for fraud and is currently being held in Prison Unit 2.

Rodolfo A. Ruiz Pizarro: Statement

Stated being of Argentine nationality, forty-seven years of age, civil status married. That he has been a painter since his youth and earns a living producing paintings that are for purely decorative purposes. That he knows of Señor Vogelius by name as a prominent collector. Asked if Señor Vogelius ever requested that he produce imitation Figaris, says this is not the case. That there is nothing more he can say on the matter.

Juan Alberto Gregorio Sabatini: Witness Statement

Bank clerk by profession. That he works as an assessor of various kinds of items at Municipal Bank. That on October 28, 1960, Señor Vogelius deposited as securities eleven full-sized paintings and seventeen smaller works, all of them oil on cardboard and original works by Pedro Figari. Señor Vogelius explained that he was in need of funds as an opportunity had arisen to acquire a painting by Georges Braque. None of the paintings were in frames, Vogelius stating that he had removed these "for ease of handling." That it is neither normal nor standard practice for such a quantity of paintings to be deposited as securities and even less so for them to be without their frames and glass.

Ernesto Deira: Witness Statement

Thirty-nine years of age, civil status married, lawyer by profession. That he is a close friend of Señor Vogelius. That he is a close friend also of Juan Fernández, who a month before going into hospital for an operation went to see the witness to make him aware of his situation and to ask him to see to certain matters of a personal nature on his behalf, furnishing him with some sealed envelopes with the request that he burn them should Fernández die, which, in February 1962, he did.

Justice Dr. H. D. Rojas Pellerano: Sentence
1968

Federico Manuel Vogelius: What lies behind this so very striking name, even the mellifluousness of which is conspicuous to those of us accustomed to the sound of Western and Latin names? Vogelius: there is a sonority to it redolent of Middle Eastern mystery. But Vogelius cannot be held responsible for the sound of his name. On the contrary, he is to be thanked, were it possible, for not being called López. In time, and once the chroniclers and memoirists have had their say, recalling him will be both easier and more romantic: the "*affaire* Vogelius" is not merely the "López case."

Everything begins with Damián Bendahan, a business associate of Vogelius, buying eleven Figari paintings.

When the business in which they are mutually involved ceases to trade, Bendahan learns that these eleven are fakes. Vogelius has made mention of one Señor Ramos as the person to whom the whole subject returns, but it is our view that this curious dealer of paintings as well as of cigarettes exists only in his imagination, given that nobody but Vogelius would appear to have any memory of him or know where he might be found. In these same years the Paris exhibition takes place, organized by Vogelius with the assistance of Señor Fernández. Twenty-eight authentic paintings leave Buenos Aires, twenty-eight counterfeit paintings come back. Vogelius protests his innocence in the matter; the only possibility is for the paintings that went to Paris, on being brought back, to have been copied at the Witcomb Gallery under the direction of Señor Fernández, who would have commissioned the counterfeiter to carry out this job at the gallery premises.

This hundred-year-old gallery is renowned as the most estimable, important, and traditional in the country. It takes quite the leap of imagination to picture Señor Fernández, the sole owner and manager, down in the basement in the company of a ne'er-do-well counterfeiter producing sham paintings. Juan Fernández has worked at the Witcomb for twenty-five years and no complaints have ever arisen.

Granted, Señor Vogelius offered to buy certain of the paintings upon returning them to some of their exhibitors, but neither we nor they can be at all sure what would have come to pass had they agreed to sell. What is clear is that said offer would have distracted the owner while also making Vogelius seemingly above suspicion and, were it to have become necessary, served as proof of Vogelius's good faith. He could conceivably have asked if the paintings were for sale, full in the knowledge that they were counterfeits, with the sole objective of creating some evidence in his own favor.

Vogelius seeks to deflect attention, naming other characters: characters such as this Señor Ramos—whereabouts unknown—and such as Juan Fernández, of less mysterious whereabouts, being that he is dead. Vogelius does not thereby demonstrate his innocence, but rather seeks to take up a position that, in his view, will have him seen as *in dubio pro reo*. Supposing that the defendant had nothing to do with the alterations to the paintings, did he, Federico Manuel Vogelius, an authority of Figari's work, at no point notice anything amiss with the paintings, each of which he returned in person? "Crude imitations," the experts called them.

Soon after the Paris exhibition, Vogelius deposited a large number of the Figari paintings at Municipal Bank as securities against a loan. Is it possible for a Figari collector to have such a large number of paintings in his possession with neither frames around them nor glass in front as protection? Is it admissible that, as he says in his statement, had some of the paintings previously been inside frames, he would have removed these purely for ease of handling? In thinking to answer this, we can look at the occasion of Vogelius coming into possession of three very valuable paintings—among them one by Francisco Goya—which had no frames; no sooner were they delivered to him than he commissioned the construction of a wooden box to house all three canvases, these to be made with all possible haste and before they were handled in any way (see Appendix #6247, the statement of the carpenter). It is striking that a person whose art collection includes more than one hundred Figaris, and the owner of a gallery in which work by Marc Chagall, no less, is on display, should need to pawn such a quantity of paintings. We have the testimony of employees at that bank as to the aberrancy of this. Simple logic would suggest that the paintings were thus unhoused because the corresponding frames had been placed around the counterfeited paintings that had been returned to their owners after the Paris exhibition.

A year later, in 1961, an exhibition of Figari's work is held at the National Museum of Fine Arts in Buenos Aires in commemoration of his birth. Juan Pedro Kramer, one of the collectors, observes that this includes copies of various of the paintings previously exhibited in Paris. Pure random chance, a bit of bad luck? Have the fake paintings been put on show without their owners being advised of the switch? Or is this all part of the plan of whoever was responsible for switching the Paris paintings? It is not unreasonable to think that this centenary exhibition closed the circle begun with the show in Paris.

Vogelius, owner of one of the largest Figari collections in Latin America, and a man far from poor—who could possibly have suspected him? If there were ever occasion to lament the written nature of our judicial proceedings, perhaps it is now: one would need to be incomparably gifted and brilliant with the pen to be able to commit to the page all that has been perceived over the course of these hearings. And even had the words been magnetically recorded, the totality of all the expressions, the telltale smiles, the subtle details, could not be reproduced.

It is our view that Federico Vogelius is the person responsible for the activities that have damned Lermon, Madariaga Anchorena, and Bendahan. The way in which he engineered the matter, his anonymous participation in keeping his name from being connected with any of it, the bungling way in which he kept hold of the paintings for longer than agreed—all is suggestive of premeditation.

Ruling: 1. The accused be remanded in custody for repeated offenses of the crime of fraud (articles 55 and 172

PORTRAIT OF AN UNKNOWN LADY

of the Penal Code). I order that 50 million pesos of his assets be frozen. 2. A warrant be issued that the defendant's properties may be searched by the authorities. 3. A warrant be issued for the arrest of the accused, Federico Manuel Vogelius.

Arrest
November 20, 1968
Federico Manuel Vogelius arrested and sent to the National Detention Institution (Unit 2).

Liberty
November 25, 1968
Vogelius released from jail.

Dr. H. Papurello: Vogelius's Lawyer
1969
Regarding the person of my client, the magistrate says that "the months during which this procedure have taken place have given me ample opportunity to get to know the accused." Notwithstanding this, in the numerous hearings to which my client has been called, I never had the opportunity to see the magistrate present there. I have serious doubts as to whether he was ever in the same place as the accused. During the judicial proceedings, at least.

Evidently, the magistrate is not in a position to make

assessments such as those he offers concerning the phonetics of my client's name, or the euphony of the "*affaire* Vogelius*,*" or the existence of a "Vogelian world." The judicial function is something far more serious. The magistrate, with such expressions, unnecessarily offends the accused, forgetting that his noble office means he may pass judgment on his peers but not insult them. In Barberis's Procedural Code it states: "When it becomes clear over the course of proceedings that he is vehemently hostile to the honorable dispensing of justice, this magistrate must be removed from the case."

In response to the magistrate's reflections concerning the difficulties of identifying this Señor Ramos, I have a number of things to say. There is in fact nothing unusual about this bearing in mind that between the time of his involvement and the date of the investigation, eight years passed. It would, in fact, have been unusual had there been more to go on. One need only recall the episode, which took place in this very court, involving a hearing with several witnesses; when the magistrate, exasperated at the inability of the person being cross-examined to remember a certain detail—something the magistrate thought he should be able to remember—this magistrate was invited by the defending counsel to go through into another room and, as a way of demonstrating the witness's sincerity, there asked whether the clerk who had been taking notes in court had a mustache or not, and the magistrate was unable to answer in spite of the fact that he saw this clerk day on day.

The magistrate, with poorly judged irony, alludes to the nonappearance of Señor Ramos and the death of Señor Fernández, as though my client should be required to capture fugitives and resuscitate the dead in order to prove his assertions. If the accusations had materialized immediately after the events under discussion, rather than eight years later, it is eminently possible that Señor Ramos would have been located and that Señor Fernández would still be alive.

Señor Vogelius is neither an art dealer nor an expert, but rather a great lover of art. Professionals in this sphere—those who make a living from their knowledge of artworks—are another matter. And even they had to resort to intricate studies before it was possible for them to pronounce on the paintings in question, and still they claimed to be lacking the "suitable evidence." For the show in Paris, the paintings were placed in crates and deposited at the Witcomb Gallery. The owners and exhibitors noticed nothing out of place when they again took possession of them. A year later, some of these same works were shown at the National Museum of Fine Arts without the organizers noticing anything (there was only one complaint), and it was another several years before the accusation arose.

In this whole inquiry, there is nothing that would allow it to be stated with any level of certainty that: 1. The paintings belonging to Lermon, Madariaga Anchorena, and Bendahan are forgeries: for the methods used by the experts are highly insufficient. 2. Had these paintings been proved to be forgeries, neither is there anything of substance to show that Señor Vogelius had a hand in their creation. 3. The elements included in the judgment do not *prima facie* demonstrate the existence of a crime. I request that my client's custody be revoked.

Statement
Judge Dionisio Pellerano removed from the case.

Miguel F. del Castillo, Investigating Judge: Ruling
1973
It is ruled that case 7569, Federico Manuel Vogelius, on repeated offenses of the crime of fraud, be dismissed, on the basis of the expiry of the statute of limitations.

Let it be noted, published, and filed.

The Virtues of the Crocodile

Nothing about Renée in the files, nothing about Lydis, but

having gone off on this tangent, there were other things

I learned. In the early 1970s Vogelius went on to set up

a publisher of art books and poetry called Dead Weight;

later sold his Chagall to finance a journal on politics and culture; was kidnapped by an army task force, escaping one night through a pig farm; went to live in London, where he fell ill, before taking refuge at a windswept health resort near Mar del Plata. In one of his last interviews he told the journalist that he was now a herbivorous lion, spending his days playing speed chess and his nights letting off fireworks on the beach. The piece appeared a week later in a political weekly and, making striking use of the first person, began thus: "It always amazes me the lengths to which people will go to resemble the legends that surround them."

It's been six days. Cooped up in this hotel, writing a report nobody asked me to write. What a thing. I have never been interested in events that take place in broad daylight, in the middle of the street, in view of all. No, such situations hold no interest for me. It is the back alley, the tucked-away place, the nook, to which I am always drawn.

> I have a key
> So I open the door and walk in.
> It is dark and I walk in.
> It is darker and I walk in.

> Mark Strand

In this life, I've encountered only one or two people like me, but I know they are out there in their scores. Last night, I listened for hours at the open window to the nasal twang of foreigners walking in the Recoleta Cemetery, passing by its mausoleums, vengeful angels, demons, and masonic obelisks—and I would have stayed in that place indefinitely, this intrauterine existence, fed, clothed—but no. The concierge today told me the room, paid for by the newspaper, was up on Sunday, and that they weren't paying the minibar bill. I mustn't forget to call the taxi-driver ninja to come and get me; I've adopted him as my personal chauffeur. And until then, I mustn't lose concentration. Hurry to the heart of this story, whatever and wherever it may be. Perhaps it will help if I bear in mind that the heart is not heart-shaped after all but rather that of an overturned pyramid . . .

Renée produced counterfeit paintings, let's suppose this much, but is insincerity really so terrible a thing? "I think not," said Oscar Wilde. "It is merely a method by which we can multiply our personalities." Perhaps all our sadness can be attributed to living trapped within ourselves. Perhaps it's only the counterfeiter who finds a way past this obstacle. Who hasn't at some time or another thought, oh, if only I were this or that person! Anyway, simulation, when it starts early, becomes part of a person's character.

•

Ricardo Becher made *Coup de Grâce* in 1969, a cult movie about the sixties based on a book of the same name by Sergio Mulet, an actor and beatnik poet known as the most beautiful man of his generation. The story centers on a group who get together at Bar Moderno—golden youth, renegade intellectuals given to making goading, grandiloquent statements like, "Got to get into something really big, get in and get out quick." A woman appears among them called Renée. The actress who plays her— Maria Vargas—is as dark and lush as chocolate fondant and I would be willing to bet that the character is based on my Renée. I went looking for the Mulet book but he's a slippery figure. I asked in the bookshops on Avenida Corrientes. Luigi, a bookseller friend of mine, said he had never seen the novel in his life. "At some point I asked Ricardo Becher, a charming guy though not the easiest to deal with, and physically a wreck, still suffering the effects of the pedestal he was placed on in his youth, and according to him the novel did exist, or it had once upon a time, until the last copy crumbled to dust in his hands."

An academic of a serious sort would have moved heaven and earth to lay their hands on the book, but by this time I'd begun to think of myself as "the indolent biographer": if the thing was going to become any more complicated, I'd simply let it go. The necessary patience wasn't a quality I possessed; I wasn't accustomed to the collating of materials and weighing up of contradictory testimonies. Fundamentally I was looking for the most vital thing, the revealing detail, nothing more. I had an excuse for my slothfulness, still do: the gaps in a life are not negative spaces that the biographer ought to feel compelled to fill; they, too, can be wellsprings, unmapped boreholes, the terra infirma where legend proliferates. When it came to Renée, evidence was thin on the ground while fables were in generous supply.

"Facts, the least useful of all superstitions," said Hâjî Abdû El-Yezdî, the mystic Sufi poet. So I went along, dowsing rod in hands, not placing much store in these dry bits of rubble which became truths merely by dint of repetition. As though truth were the be-all and end-all and not just another well-told story. But finally, not even my dowsing techniques were bringing decent results. I had, to be exact, less than nothing to show for myself. An image: this beautiful, enigmatic, talented woman, supposedly the country's greatest counterfeiter, who one day disappeared without a trace. In material terms, that was about it. The only forged painting I'd seen with my own eyes, the one at the Hotel Melancholical, had a certificate of authenticity—it could very well not have been a forgery at all. Beyond that, a couple of voluble octogenarians who'd insisted on trotting out anecdotes and who afterward kept on calling me, on any pretext, to chat about the past, which is to say, about themselves. It was while burning the midnight oil with them that I began to see how a biography is, by its very nature, something ineffable. People don't remember very much, sometimes not even what they had for breakfast that morning. Reality is perhaps a thing too inherently ruinous for there to be any abiding certainty about it.

He came to my house one day; he was short and had a knowing glint in his eye. He was handsome, but with the kind of good looks one isn't sure will last. Martín was thirty years old and an expert on marginal Argentinean writers from the 1960s. The opening exchanges were about each of us gauging our opponent; every encounter begins with some probing. It was obvious that he held all the cards, being the one who had known her. He was, by my calculations, the last person to have seen her alive.

"It would have been five years ago," he said. "She made a living growing cactuses—her way of having contact with people. Her house was like some favela shack—bottles, boxes, bits of metal all over the place, the sort of squalor that's reached the point of no return. She had a kitchen, a living room, her bedroom, and a fourth room which she told me I mustn't go into because, she said, it was in a complete state after a recent flood—really, I thought, the whole house was in a complete state. See how that is? Someone says, don't go through a certain door, and suddenly the only thing you want to do is open it. I went around once and, while she was getting herself out of bed and so on, I took my chance, had a look. The moment I opened the door, the rancid air inside hit me, as though there was something rotting in there, and then I saw a bed with a filthy mattress and a chair with a plastic food container and what I thought looked like putrid meat inside. I then heard her footsteps coming down the hall, and dashed back to where I'd been sitting. I could have sworn that as I went to close the door I saw a scaly tail poking out from under the bed, but it could have been auto-suggestion; I'd heard the stories. I never mentioned it, but she knew without having to ask. She was no witch, no way; in fact, she hated magic and superstition; according to her, to believe in any of that was the same as believing in power, and power was the enemy of art. But she also liked giving people a fright. One day I asked if she'd ever killed anybody and she kicked me out straight away—insisted I leave, anyway, since she was very old by that time and one of her knees was really wrecked. What she did have was incredible energy for her age. 'If I were forty years younger I'd give you a good seeing to,' she said. When I met her she was painting portraits but, she said, not doing forgeries anymore. She gave me a drawing once as a gift, a charcoal portrait of Kafka, but later on changed her mind and asked for it back. When I said no, it was mine now, she threatened to come to my house with stones in her pockets and smash everything up. That didn't happen, of course, because she never went out.

"She talked to me a lot about her forgeries. She kept old newspaper cuttings whenever any of her paintings appeared, circling them in red pen. The signature, she always said, was the hardest part. She later moved house and I lost track of her. I don't know where she might be now, but you ought to hurry, she struggled in winter. It's strange nobody had any photos—did you ask Rómulo? He's got Iaros's archive."

I thought this had to be the plover's trick: Martín was also hoping to write about Renée and was calling far from the nest to throw me off. But at the same time it could have been an honest suggestion, good intentions. That was also a possibility—why not.

Renée would have been around eighty at that time and was still painting, although no longer doing forgeries; she had cut herself off from the world, and a counterfeiter needs contacts. I returned to my questions. What if Renée's legend exceeded her talent? Perhaps she wasn't the painter people claimed her to be, perhaps she'd turned to forgeries out of a dissatisfaction with her own work. Out of being overdemanding? Indifferent? Or was it more than simply a question of art? That Renée was just a con artist full stop? That the whole thing was just some elaborate *mise en-abîme*? Perhaps she had forged the occasional painting, but seen from the vantage of the present day, those one or two seemed like thousands. Perhaps Renée was the most normal person in the world. There is a D. J. Enright poem that goes: "Much easier than your works / To sell your quirks."

The white-haired man who opened the door to me would have been disappointed to find before him not a show-stopping beauty but skinny little me wrapped in my black fur coat. Being the gentleman that he was, he made no complaint and got quickly to the reason I'd come. He was a painter, one of the few remaining from the era in which painting was still a matter of grand gestures.

"I've got them somewhere." This was what the man calling himself Rómulo said to me. He got up from his chair, went and pulled open a drawer. "They're actually where they're supposed to be, miraculously."

Some fifty photographs in black and white were now spread out on a low round table in the painter's very modern home. They had been taken by Iaros, a photographer whose named I'd heard mentioned, being one of the Hotel Melancholical cohort. Iaroslav Kosak, the Ukrainian with the face of a fox and his briefcase always about his person. Rómulo had been fifteen when he first met him at the local gym and fencing club, where they both practiced judo. Their paths crossed again at Bar Moderno in the late sixties, but Iaros was at a different table with his dancer-philosopher girlfriend. One day, the girl said she was leaving him. This story, with certain variations, is included in a book by Juan José Sebreli and in a short story by Bernardo Kordon. That night, Iaros ran a bath and waited for her to come home. When she arrived, he hoisted her up, plunged her into the bath, and held her head under the water. By the time the police came, the bath was empty, the floor dry, and Iaros was sitting stroking his dog with a Chopin concerto on in the background. Rómulo was already installed in La Boca when the Ukrainian moved to the area; he had been acquitted of the crime, but lost his apartment and now slept in a homeless shelter. The painter found him one sunset in a dive down at the port, where Iaros spent his time inveighing against André Kertész, who according to him had stolen some of his tricks. The only thing he got on with were very tiny dogs, the kind that run in circles between their owners' feet like circus horses. Rómulo heard his doorbell ring very early one morning. It was one of Iaros's bar mates. "The Ukrainian's been dragged off to the asylum," he said. "They took him in the clothes he stood in, impounded the camera and everything." A small suitcase of photographs had been left behind under his bed. Could he look after them? A while later, someone saw Iaros in Alvear Hospital giving conferences to the patients, talking about how he'd been John Ford's director of photography . . .

"But to go back to your questions."

The surviving photographs from that suitcase were there in front of me. I spent some time over them; they were all black and white, none of them particularly artistic or with any pretensions to being documentary, lots featuring bars from the 1960s, some Avenida Corrientes, some the Salada baths. I couldn't see how they were going to be of any use to me, and my retractable heart drew back in exasperation. Rómulo was patting down his hair—I said before that it was white but I ought also to have clarified that it had a springiness to it too—and I was about to thank him and leave when I saw his right hand reach forward over the untidy heap of pictures. Suddenly it stopped, descended, moved a couple of the photographs aside, and picked one out from the swirling mass of them. I held my breath like when the fairground grabber claw comes up with the best of all the cuddly toys.

"There," he said. "There's your girl, Renée."

•

I confess I had come to a point of thinking that she didn't actually exist, was rather a product of a group flight of fancy, a collective delirium, the dream of an entire generation—perpetuated in countless stories, passed like Chinese whispers down to later generations, morphing all the way. But reality is both stranger than fiction and more diffuse and, now that I think of it, no drug exists that is capable of inducing such a fantasy in so many different individuals. All the sciences agree. Only life has the obstinacy of the gambling addict: the stubbornness to throw the dice as many times as needed before one exceptional individual appears in our midst.

"There she is," said Rómulo once more.

The photo was slightly out of focus, taken from a distance like a paparazzi shot. A man and a woman are walking down what could be Avenida Corrientes. They are passing a poster for Colorado cigarettes, the "l" in which is giving off smoke like some hyperbolic take on their impassioned state. They are walking along arguing, the photo catching them in a pause; a few minutes later they'll go back to talking again, the conversation taking them down another black hole. Behind them is a flower stall, but it's no moment for flowers. He looks like a standard Buenos Aires man, a little in the style of Philip Marlowe, shirt and tie, hands thrust in pockets, oppressed-looking, brow knitted. But I had already met him—it was her I was interested in. This Valkyrie incongruously stuffed into a tailored dress, her black hair cut short, flat nose, calves of steel. Her carriage upright and her arms crossed. She would have been about thirty. Disappointment had been very much on the cards, but no: she had exactly the correct *physique du rôle*. It was Renée.

"Everyone wanted to be with her," said Rómulo, giving a deep exhalation—sighing, a poet would say.

Renée had given up on the world, or the world had given up on Renée? There was a story one of the hotel guests had told me:

"In a river in Africa that runs from Sierra Leone out to the Atlantic, there once lived a crocodile with dazzlingly bright skin. To protect itself from the sun's rays, the creature spent its days down in the muddy riverbed, and rarely ever came out. But then one night it decided to do so. To begin with, being suspicious by nature, it kept to the sandy shore, not moving an inch, jaws open wide to waft away the unpleasant taste of the heat and three-quarters of its tail still in the water—primed to slide back into the river at any movement it didn't like the look of. A watchful owl was the first to notice its presence. In its alarm, it joked to one of its neighbors on a branch above:

"'Look,' it said, 'there's something strange over there.'

MARÍA GAINZA

"'What?' said the other, eyes wide as plates.

"'Can't you see?' it said. 'There's a light.'

"'Stop trying to scare me.'

"They called all of the owls together, and a great noise went up as the mass of them gathered, hooting to one another: What is it? An evil light? Go and have a look! What, are you crazy, *you* go look! In the end only one old, taciturn owl went to see, and, putting its wings over its eyes to avoid being blinded, went tottering toward the light.

"'Oo-hoo!' sighed the old owl in amazement. 'It's a crocodile, a crocodile of dazzling brightness!'

"'Oo-h-hoo!' went the cry through the rest of the forest.

"And, soothed by this adulation, swelling with pride, the crocodile started coming out of the water at all hours. So it was that for a time, in Sierra Leone, the only topic of conversation was how lovely the crocodile was, beauty being a thing so devilishly seductive that it has the capacity to override moral questions. But days went by, and the idyll among the forest animals and the crocodile began, inevitably, to deteriorate. In specific: the crocodile's skin started to turn dull from exposure to the sun, and a month later it became rough, too, coarse to the touch, and then, from one day to the next, dried out completely and lost all its former sparkle. All the animals were disappointed and returned to their usual activities, while the crocodile went bitterly back to the bottom of the river. Since then it has only ever poked its eyes above the water, like a couple of periscopes, watching out while keeping the rest of itself hidden."

What a delightful waste of time my quest had proven to be up to this point! A pathetic biography whose lack of resolution I found strangely gratifying. It was the photo that set off the alarm. It made me feel like the lover who wants to know everything about his beloved, even while he realizes that this curiosity carries within itself the seed of disappointment. "Is this all love is?" Julien Sorel asked himself, the first time he spent a night with a woman.

And yes, that was all it was. What had I imagined? That a month from then, in two years, or ten, I would find my way to a house in some Buenos Aires suburb, cross a shady patio with a dozen cats prowling about, and pound on the door with the heavy knocker? That there would come the tip-tap of high heels, the jangle of keys as one turned in the lock, and finally the door would swing open?

"I've been expecting you," a woman of indecipherable age would say to me, a toughness about her like Michelangelo's Delphic Sibyl. The rest would come naturally and at some point in our uncomplicated conversation I would ask—with neither drama nor emotion—the questions I've been carrying around all this time. You know: whether it's certain that good and evil dance around every single electron, whether it is better to be the lichen on a rock than a president's carnation, whether what we do matters but we do not.

But none of this would come to pass. I had only imagined it because I had read the same scene, though with variations, in something Jill Johnston wrote about the lost painter Agnes Martin.

One chooses one's totem and one sticks with it. It happens with writers and those on whom they write biographies, and with people and their pets as well. As a girl I went to the zoo to see the *aguará guazú*, the maned wolf, but the animal refused to come out. Then, on what would have been my sixth time there, it finally appeared. It crossed from left to right in an instant, before the yellow flowers of the Jerusalem thorn swallowed it like a portal to another dimension. How strange, I thought, it looks nothing like the *aguará guazú*. When I say "Renée" now, I know that the figure sketched on the chalkboard of my mind is a distortion. Characters with precisely wrought histories, linear psychologies, and coherent ways of

behaving are one of literature's great fallacies. We have little and nothing: only what we are today, at a stretch what
we did yesterday, and with luck what we're going to do
tomorrow. This needs to be borne in mind when thinking
of Renée and, after that, she has to be let go of, because
to find her would be to ruin something that I have been
unable to define but nonetheless intuit as important. So it
was that one day I promised myself that I would give up
searching for her.

The Checkout

It was one of those e-mails so oppressively full of exclama-

tion marks and words in italics and bold, that one deletes

it from the in-box without so much as reading it. And

yet something in it drew my eye: the word "medium,"

perhaps. The press release announced a session at the Roca Museum run by a Brazilian man who claimed to be able to contact the spirits of the impressionists. Saying to myself that I didn't know enough about the unknown to state categorically that it was unknowable, I decided to take the plunge. *The Godfather* had said it already: Just when I thought I was out, they pull me in.

Rogelio Nori, with his dark skin and bulging biceps under a tight-fitting polo shirt, spoke like a used-car salesman and claimed to have a hyperdeveloped pineal gland, and that this allowed him direct access to the spirits of great fin-de-siècle painters. Not only could Nori communicate with them, he could also let them enter his body and control what he did. A specialism defined in Kardec's *The Spirits' Book* as "medium pictography."

The Rationalist building that houses the Roca is in Recoleta, a stone's throw from the cemetery. When I arrived, the events space was wall-to-wall with people. I found a chair with green leather upholstery and sat down, my fingers interlaced spider-like on my thighs. The red velvet curtains at the back of the stage shielded the full-body portrait of Julio Argentino Roca, twice president of Argentina. The weight, the very anvil of history, was strongly present. But something made it an unstable equilibrium.

"The spirits started when I was eight," Nori began.

"They messed up my bed, threw things on the floor, I could see them clear as daylight—like I can see all of you here right now. When I told this to a nun, she said it was the Devil's work. But sister, I said, the spirits, they tell me to get down on my knees and pray. Child, she said, the Devil has a thousand masks.

"One day the spirits told me to go and get a piece of paper. I sat down, shut my eyes, felt all nervous, excited—I lost control. I did ten paintings with signatures I knew nothing about. Renoir came to me like the foreman for the whole thing, it was he who said: 'You aren't going to have the chance to study painting, far better to let others be your guide.' Next up Degas appears, tells me to go and buy pastels—I thought he meant 'pasteles,' cakes.

"Might our greatest painters be looking out for the lighthouse of a gifted medium, a way of continuing their work while they sail on through the ocean of eternity?"

Nori's talk ended there, followed by him putting on his smock.

A pair of blushing assistants in white overalls brought out a canvas and placed it on a lectern. The medium shut his eyes and began mouthing a silent rhapsody or invocation. I was slightly concerned that ectoplasm was going to make an appearance, that viscous, mozzarella-like substance of which I had seen some pictures, but then his lips parted to paint a beatific smile on his face. This was followed by Nori going into a frenzy, though I don't know if that's the precise word because really it looked as though he had cramps; was this him being used as a conduit? Suddenly his expression changed, he stopped what he was doing and looked around; a woman in the audience had opened a packet of candy and the rustling of the wrapper had distracted him. He asked for there to be silence, making a throat-slitting gesture with one finger; a detail that suggested to me Nori's strength of character, as well as startling me, though it also struck me as a good thing that, however far the medium might go, he wouldn't leave his head behind—keeping it with him I supposed so he would be fully aware of his own derangement. The woman postponed the sugar hit and the medium went back to what he had been doing. This time one of the assistants placed a brush in his hand and Nori launched himself at the canvas.

Five minutes had gone by, in the normal passage of time, when the man collapsed on the stage. At which the assistants, perfectly choreographed, spun the canvas around for the audience to see. A deep exhalation was heard throughout the room, the kind that is followed by all the ambient dirt and muck entering the lungs. Before us was a Renoir. A vase with flowers by Renoir, quality debatable perhaps, but when all was said and done, a Renoir.

There was no time for any nitpicking, however, as he was back on his feet already and had set about a new blank canvas. But this time, when he was done, the general exhalation was less effusive. It was a Sisley. Sisley on a bad day. The worst day of his life. A day when Sisley had woken up with liver pains and subcapsular cataracts.

By this point I was thinking about how one would go about distinguishing a false medium from an authentic medium if even a true medium could be deceived by false spirits. And while I tried to keep my cynicism in check, the woman in front of me, elderly and with generous amounts of hair spray, turned and, as though she had read my mind, gave me a mascara-daubed wink.

What a relief this was—I wasn't the only one! It was like being in Las Vegas at one of the Siegfried and Roy shows with the flying tigers. Nobody dared ask whether it was all a hoax. In that place, everyone wanted to believe. Because in the face of this man, the world had an order: there was a here and a there, a place beyond, and in between them a channel, a tunnel, a corridor, a bandwidth, a stairway to heaven—whatever we chose to name it. A passageway connecting the two worlds, and if you were to reach out, stretching your arm fully, your forefinger could brush that of the hand reaching through from the opposite side.

I left the Roca Museum and walked a number of blocks alongside the Recoleta Cemetery; there was a strong wind blowing and I went head-on into it like some Winged Victory of Samothrace, clothes blown taut against my body and dress streaming out on all sides. But there was a smile on my face, thinking of all the people like me there must have been at the session, solitary travelers in their own bubbles of time, missing contact with old friends.

The wind blew and blew. And with it went everything inside my head.

Knocking on the door. The concierge calls out, reminding me checkout is at 11 a.m. He can wait; I need to turn out the pockets of my heart, shake them until the last little ten-centavo coin falls to the floor.

What drove me in this search? Was it only an attempt to stop myself from collapsing? Was it curiosity? The ecstasy of discovery? None of these answers satisfies me. When someone beloved dies, the reflex is basic and, I sense, universal: someone goes back mentally over this person, examining topics discussed, salvaging the old lexicon of nudges and shared jokes, revising the places you had in common. One doesn't do so out of masochism, but to keep that person alive, "to keep the ball rolling," as Conrad said, because one day the person you love above everyone else disappears and you realize that the conversation has been cut short. In these moments, it isn't the nice memories we ask the past to produce for us; any memory at all will suffice, more than suffice. In essence I think that I came up with this quest as a way of going on talking with my old friend Enriqueta; given that I could no longer accompany her to the sauna, or remove the bones from the fish on her plate, given that I could no longer hand her the black light like a burning torch, the words were at least a way of cleaving to her. So I came up with a topic of conversation: we talked about Renée.

More knocking. A few minutes until I give up this Imperial Room of mine. I read a number of pages from my report, before putting it away somewhere safe: in those pages, a gallery of characters cross paths—through fate or pure luck—in a certain moment in history. They display, like the setting in which they arise, the unstable quality of an apparition. But I'm under no illusions: they aren't ghosts, because ghosts don't have any hearts; they are normal, run-of-the-mill mortals, who like me have to put up with both the suffocating atmosphere of reality and the rarefied air of dreams. Out of all of them, Renée is the only one who approximates an immortal being, an angel or a demon from the *Paradise Lost* illustrated by Blake.

Strange: It has come to me that one doesn't write to remember, or to forget, or to find relief, or to cure oneself of some pain. One writes to plumb one's own depths, to understand what's inside. At least, so it is in what I've written, as though an endoscope were making its way through my body. I know I run the risk of going down as a sycophant. I see it already: they will accuse me of high treason, point me out in the street, handing down their disdainful verdict. In my defense, I will echo Marina Tsvetaeva and say, "Calumny is the self-portrait of the calumniator," and I am the first to admit I have had my hand slopping around in the mud. Believe me, mud is restorative and a tonic.

I take a last look under the bed. A ballpoint pen lies on the green carpet. I get down on the floor, reach out an arm, there it is, I have it. And now I am chewing on the point of the pen, looking at the report in my paper bag and thinking, with some satisfaction, that the thing it contains is worth preserving. This, I suppose, explains the calm that has come over me these past days. So it is, we human beings are made of elements old and simple: carbon, hydrogen, oxygen, and nitrogen.

Some months after I left the paper, the young critic quit in order to become a curator. The ceiling in criticism is low, and he was a man of elevated stature. The editor on the arts desk begged me to go back: "Nobody wants to write about art anymore," she implored. I don't know if she knew how unseductive this was as an argument. I could have taken refuge in my resentment, but what an outrageous waste of energy that would have been! Better to just go back to the aridity of my reviews; after all, those weekly deadlines had, in their moment, been the only thing to keep me on an even keel. I accepted, and only time—even if there is no such thing—would tell if I'd done the right thing.

So I have come to be at the Hotel Étoile, with its charm, its faded glamour. In this room, gathering myself for my return. This has also meant I've kept my promise, giving up my search these months past, which isn't to say I don't still think about her. She comes to mind with some regularity.

Just like that, out of nowhere, Renée appears to me, and when she does I ask myself: Will she be dead now?

Only to shoo away the idea like a fly. No, I say to myself, there's far too much life in her for that.

MARÍA GAINZA was born in Buenos
Aires, where she still resides. She is the author of
Optic Nerve, which was a *New York Times* Notable
Book and a finalist for the Los Angeles Times Book
Prize's Art Seidenbaum Award for First Fiction.
She has worked as a correspondent for *The New
York Times* in Argentina, as well as for *ARTnews*.
She has also been a contributor to *Artforum*, *The
Buenos Aires Review*, and *Radar*, the cultural supple-
ment from the Argentinean newspaper *Página/12*.
She is coeditor of the collection *Los Sentidos* (The
Senses) on Argentinean art, and in 2011 she pub-
lished *Textos elegidos* (Selected Texts), a collection
of her notes and essays on contemporary art.

THOMAS BUNSTEAD has translated some of the leading Spanish-language writers working today, including Bernardo Atxaga, Agustín Fernández Mallo, and Enrique Vila-Matas, and his own writing has appeared in such publications as *Brixton Review of Books*, *Literary Hub*, and *The White Review*. He is currently a Royal Literary Fellow teaching at Aberystwyth University. He was born in London and now lives in Pembrokeshire, Wales.